This Is the World

This Is the World

W. S. Penn

Michigan State University Press · *East Lansing*

♾ The paper used in this publication meets the minimum requirements
of ANSI/NISO Z39.48–1992 (R 1997) (Permanence of Paper).

Michigan State University Press
East Lansing, Michigan 48823-5202

Printed and bound in the United States of America.

07 06 05 04 03 02 01 00   1 2 3 4 5 6 7 8 9 10

LIBRARY OF CONGRESS CATALOGING-IN-PUBLICATION DATA
Penn, W. S., 1949–
This is the world / W. S. Penn.
p.   cm.
ISBN 0-87013-561-9 (pbk. : alk. paper)
1. United States—Social life and customs—20th century—Fiction.
2. Indians of North America—Fiction. I. Title.
PS3566.E476 T48 2000
813'.54—dc21
00-008702

ACKNOWLEDGMENTS
Many of these stories appeared in the following magazines: *Antaeus, Bananas* (U.K.),
Missouri Review, the *Northern Review, Quarterly West, Stand* (U.K.), *Southern Humanities
Review, Tangent* (U.K.), the *Vanderbilt Review,* and the *Vanderbilt Street Press.* To their edi-
tors and editorial boards, and to the judges of the Iowa Prize (who made the collection a
finalist one year), as well as to the New York Foundation for the Arts, thank you.

Cover design by Ariana Grabec-Dingman
Book design by Sharp Des!gns, Lansing, Michigan
Cover artwork is "Untitled" and is used courtesy of the artist, Anthony Siani

Visit Michigan State University Press on the World Wide Web at:
www.msu.edu/unit/msupress

Dedicated to George P. Elliott

Writer, Friend, and Teacher

Contents

This Is the World

I.

THERE WAS A TIME WHEN I WAS LIGHTHEARTED. AN IDEALIST, I GUESS. At least people had called me that: "Idealist!" they'd say, as though they were saying, "Sonuvabitch."

And they were right. I was. I wasn't ashamed. What's wrong with having ideals? Does it mean you're impractical? And so what if it does? John Dewey was not a happy man. Mark Twain was, although embittered at the end.

Being an idealist means most often that you're poor. You're poor because you cannot see the joy of pushing memos around an office or the pleasure in strip-mining Pike's Peak. Being poor isn't as much fun as the politicians and the rich seem to think.

Furthermore, being poor wastes a tremendous amount of time. You have to plan out your meals each week so you can afford to eat seven out of seven days. When you discover ground meat has gone up again, you have to stop and think about where you can trim your budget. You stand in drugstores to read magazines; you deliberate for days not just about whether you can afford a movie but also about which movie to see (see a bad one, and you can't afford the good one that will open as soon as you've spent the money on the bad one). You have to spend hours in line waiting to fill out forms that have been designed to cause mistakes, so you have to get back in line to get new forms—in order to apply for a job or to receive welfare. The worst thing about being poor is that, to listen to the politicians and their non-poor constituents, you don't exist.

The rich exist. You bet. If you don't believe me just ask any poor person. Ask a Vietnamese, or a Colombian, or a Salvadorean. Or if you're a simple person, observe the meat counter at your local super. See the woman piling sirloin into the cart? She works for the rich. Or she is newly rich herself and has yet to learn how it's done.

With these things and more in mind, I decided to put off the cloak of poverty, to lay aside my ideals, and to join the legion of the rich.

I began with the barber. No, he was second. First came my father. I wrote him: "Guess what, Dad? I'm going to get a job."

He wrote right back. He approved heartily. "Dear Son Albert," he wrote. "Now you can buy life insurance. You will have retirement. You can pay taxes, buy a car, buy car insurance (be sure to get coverage for uninsured drivers), buy a house and get mortgage insurance, fire insurance, theft insurance, insurance against Acts of God and Congress, buy dental, medical, and optometrical insurance. I'm proud of you, son. Love, Albert your dad."

Think of it!

Then the barber. He wasn't immediately approving, but I won him over with my cheerful practicality.

"I don't cut ——— hippie's hair," he said.

I explained that I wished to have it cut off so I could get a job.

"Off?" he said. He had eyes like black marbles. They seemed to light up the way a cat's will when the light is right. "Off?" he said again.

"Yes," I said. "Practically. Just over the ears. Can you do that?"

I could see the idea gave him pleasure. From years as a welder repairing rotten seams on tanks, I knew the look he gave me—or my hair, sizing it up. The challenge. The correction of something that had been allowed to go to pot.

I listened carefully in the chair while he tried his barber's talk out on me. Had I heard Sugar Ray was gonna fight in the Dome? Sugar Ray sounded like a candy bar and I had no idea what the Dome was—but I was determined to learn, so I said, "Yeah. That'll be something, won't it?"

"Something," he said. "Sure will. I'll say it'll be something. Ray'll kill him."

God, I hope not, I thought, and said, "Yeah. Boy, I'd sure hate to go up against old Sugar Ray."

The barber laughed. I'd made him happy.

Then it was baseball. I know even less about that, so I listened more carefully.

"See where Dippy Jensen's hitting .356?" he said. "Is he on a streak, eh? Beginning of the season that sucker was hitting .230. Couldn't hit the broad side of a barn."

I'd caught on. "Couldn't hit a pregnant cow if it was standing still," I said. Long locks of my hair fell across the apron. The barber looked at me warily in the mirror. "But .356, that's something," I said. He began cutting again. I took a chance. "Say, that was sad about that ballplayer getting killed," I said. Someone was always getting killed. Odds favored one being a ballplayer.

"Who got killed?" he said. Wary again.

But I was learning. "Last year. Or maybe it was the year before."

"Oh," he said. He wiped his eye with the back of his hand. "Oh, you mean Munson. Yeah. Jeez, that was awful. What a way to go. Good ballplayer."

"Yeah," I said. "Sad."

"I know what you mean." With immense feeling, he lifted my hair and lopped it off. I could see him reach down inside for a cheerier topic—I have always suspected the non-poor don't like too much sadness in conversation. Can't we talk about something happier? they'd say.

"Say," the barber said. "Wasn't that something when the hostages got home?"

"Oh, yes," I said.

"I almost cried," he said, "when I saw it on television. I admit that. I just about cried like a baby. It was something. Just . . . well, something. Nearly cried."

"Me, too."

"You watch it?"

"Yeah." I didn't own a TV. But I will, I thought.

"There," he said. He swiveled the chair around so I faced the nearer wall of mirrors. He held up a large hand mirror behind my head. "You look good now," he said, "don't you think?"

The hand mirror had Oriental dragons on the back. Rhinestones spelled U.S.S. something or other. A souvenir? He swiveled me around a second time and lifted the apron by its corners, cradling all my former hair in its folds.

The barber smiled as I paid him. Looked at me as though I were his best creation. I tipped him and walked out into the spring wind. There were young people strolling up and down the street, arm in arm or laughing. Some of them carried big tape decks and were blissfully listening to music. Even the meter maid hummed a light air as she wrote out parking tickets. The wind felt chilly on my neck, but I was happy. This was the world and I was part of it. ".356," I said. "Sugar Ray."

A quick stop at an instant-credit clothing store for a sport coat and slacks. It was too easy. As I listened to the tailor's complaints, I felt I was really branching out, my education completing itself as H-O becomes water, naturally. That night I read *Reader's Digest* to polish off the day and fell asleep quickly, repeating import quotas on Taiwanese cloth, thinking about the Dome, the rise in violent crime, etc.—untroubled by ideals.

The day for my big interview arrived and I rose happily and practiced my practical smile. So easy. By then my neck had gotten used to the feel of its nakedness; my mind had even begun to adjust to people not staring at me.

As I waited in the anteroom for my appointment, I thumbed through magazines and practiced conversations I had learned. A woman in a tight skirt came in and told me that Mr. Frank would see me now.

I'd been afraid he'd be old. He wasn't. We were about the same age, although sometimes I feel as old as my grandfather. I guessed he'd worked for this company for at least a decade. He had that air about him. I handed him my referral slip from the agency, smiling.

His name was Frank, Henry Frank of Personnel. He didn't beat around any bushes. I was trying to remember the name of the ballplayer. He asked me why I wanted to work for Syrachem.

"I need a job," I said. "I've decided to put aside my ideals and take control of my life. Work, like everyone else." Exist, I thought.

His pupils dilated. "Ideals?"

"I always wanted to be a ballplayer," I said.

"Ah," he said. "You meant dreams, not ideals."

Whatever. "Yes. Dreams. Thank you. I used to dream of being like Sugar Ray. I've faced facts now."

Mr. Frank toyed with his upper lip as though he had a mustache. He shuffled through the application forms I'd filled out, and then through some computer printouts of tests I'd taken the day before. Practical-knowledge questions. Some about what to do in emergencies. Fortunately the tests had been multiple choice. My answers would have been "Run" or "Begin to scream." With multiple choice, though, you can spot their correct answers. The less interesting ones. The calm, quiet, Dewey ones.

Mr. Frank blinked and reshuffled the papers a second time. I sensed he was looking for something he might have missed. "Do you know what we do here, Mr. Bird?" he asked.

"'Humming,'" I said.

"What?"

"My name. 'Hummingbird.'"

"Yes," he said. "I know. It says here, 'Mr. Humming Bird.'"

"No," I said. "My last name. My last name is Hummingbird." I ran the three syllables together. "My first name is Albert."

"Oh." He suppressed a laugh. "I see, now. I'm sorry. You see, the computer left off your first initial 'A' and printed it 'Humming Bird.' I thought that was odd. You see, we print only the first initials on applications. It should have read 'H. Bird' if your first name were Humming. We do that to avoid discrim . . . but never mind." He grew serious for a moment.

"I'll correct it," he said. "I'm very sorry."

"It's okay," I said.

"Yes. Yes, it should read 'A. Hummingbird.'" Then he did laugh. Through the smoked-glass partition, I could see the heads of secretaries turning toward his cubicle. He pulled out a handkerchief and dabbed his eyes. He was still chuckling when he said, "Oh, heavens. I'm very very sorry." He stopped and took three deep breaths. "It's really disgraceful, my laughing. I hope you won't take it ill."

"It's okay," I said. "I really don't mind."

"Well," he said, folding the papers into a manila envelope. "I see no reason why you can't start with us on Monday, Mr. Hummingbird." He paused. "Tell me, though," he said. "How did it feel to cut your hair?"

Did it show?

I realized he had a snapshot of me from the agency. "Good," I said. He didn't believe me. "You have to grow up sometime," I said. He still seemed bothered by my picture. "I want to buy life insurance," I said.

"Why don't I take you downstairs. Show you around. Introduce you to your new supervisor."

In the elevator he reopened my file and looked at the picture. I decided to try one last time. "Say, that was something, wasn't it, when the hostages arrived home? I nearly cried," I said. "Almost cried like a baby."

He closed the file and looked at me with approval. "Yes," he said. "A great day in American history." He took out his handkerchief and blew his nose.

That was how I used to see the world.

II.

LET ME TELL YOU WHAT I LEARNED, WORKING FOR SYRACHEM. MY JOB was easy—easier than being poor, anyway, and simpler than filling out forms for the unemployment people. I ran a pallet lift. I was on the retake end of things. Most people pulled or measured stock, packaged it, and sent it carefully on its way through a maze of conveyor belts which carried it to the right floor and section, where whatever it was was used to develop new products. Now and then a canister, some lead, some plain metal, came down the retake conveyor. My job was to wait for these canisters and cautiously move them out to the far end of the docks and load them on trucks according to the color code on their tops. What could be easier? Sometimes as few as one an hour came down. Though there were busier days.

I set out to win the approval of my fellow workers. At 10 A.M. we all gathered around on pallets and boxes or the stopped conveyors, ate jelly doughnuts, and batted the breeze. I listened, holding on to my supply of barber talk until I needed it, adding all the while to my new vocabulary.

"You hear they want to hire more nigs?" Stuart said. Stuart was thin, forty-five, lived with his mother, and, according to the talk when

7

he wasn't around, still a virgin. He took pride in being the first to punch in on our shift in the mornings and the last to punch out at night. It was his joy and no one ever tried to sneak out after him.

"Over my dead body," Andy said. "I ain't gonna work with no niggers." Andy had tattoos up and down his arms, and I'd won his favor the first week by smiling and saying, "That's something," when he showed me how "Betty" danced when he flexed his muscles in a certain way.

So I felt safe in saying, "We work with Johnson, don't we?" Johnson was a section boss.

"What's it to you," Stuart said. He seemed hostile.

"Come on, Stu," Andy said. "The kid's new." He turned to me and explained. "Johnson was in the navy. He's different from the rest of 'em."

"Yeah," Stuart said. "Navy man."

"Oh," I said.

"Ain't the marines," Andy said. "Still, it's okay."

I tried to make it up to Stuart at lunchtime. "How about this Dippy Jensen?" I said. "Hitting .356."

"It's .326. He's slumping. Where you been?"

I ate my lunch in silence after that. Still, as I was punching out, Stuart came up to me. "Here, Kid," he said, handing me a rolled-up magazine. "You can have this. It'll rest your eyes." It was a girlie magazine. Andy smiled.

I was accepted. If you were in with Stuart and Andy, you were in with everyone—Lee, Bobby, Coker, Connie, Sammie, all of them. Even Mr. Frank noticed after a month or two when he came down to see how I was getting on. "You've made quite a hit in this underworld," he said. "I asked where Albert was and nobody knew who you were till Andy came up and said, 'He means the Kid,' and everybody lit up. 'Oh, the Kid,' everybody said. So that's what they call you?" Mr. Frank said.

That was yours truly. I slept easily and well at night. I drank beer and watched my new television. In the market I shoved the rich aside and loaded my cart with choice cuts. I wrote my father for advice on insurance, and even looked over a few houses for sale. I felt like a kid again, too—youthful, hopeful, with the brashness it takes to live a decent, honest, practical life. Twain be damned, I thought. It's much easier without ideals. Reading *Reader's Digest* or the girlie magazines Stuart passed on to me left me untroubled, without worry, thoughtless. I even began to punch in in the mornings right after Stuart.

So what went wrong?

Syrachem—Mr. Frank—hired a man named Cecil Xuan. Cecil was brought down as I had been and introduced around. Mr. Frank brought him over to me. "Cecil," he said, "meet Albert, otherwise known as the Kid. Kid, watch out for Cecil, will you?"

"Sure," I said. To me, it was a sign of approval to be asked this— like getting my nickname. Besides, Cecil's job was to dolly the drums and canisters onto the trucks. There were going to be a lot of them coming down retake and he was to help me. Fine.

Things went pretty much the same and I didn't notice that some of the fellows pulled back a bit from me. We were too busy. Truck after truck drove away from the docks, and Cecil and I were often tired enough to rest and eat our lunch out at the end of the docks rather than leg it back up to the warehouse where everyone else was. I liked Cecil. He was small but very wiry. He never complained and the trucks pulled away on time.

Cecil seemed to like me okay, too. One day he sat down on the dock next to me for lunch. He poured out some stuff from his thermos and offered it to me to taste.

"What is it?" It was clear like a martini.

"Try," he said.

I did. It was pretty good. He smiled. "Rice wine," he said.

"Good. But I'm not sure we should be drinking at lunchtime, Ceece, what with these canisters. Got to be careful."

"Always drink," he said. "Keep away worms."

"Worms?"

He nodded as though he were giving away classified information. He patted his stomach. "Also cure Westmoreland's Revenge."

I wasn't so sure about all this. But at home in the peace of studying my box scores and watching TV while eating a huge steak, I forgot about it.

The next day, Cecil offered me more wine. He'd brought a larger thermos and an extra cup. I drank. I didn't want to offend him.

"You're not white," he said one day.

"What makes you say that, Ceece?" I'm not. My mother was, but my father was a halfbreed. Still, I have brown hair and skin that turns dark only on exposure to the sun.

"I can tell," he said. He tapped his index finger on my chest.

"That's something," I said. "You're right. My last name's Humming-bird."

"They don't know," he said. He pointed at the warehouse. "Inside." He looked out at the gate where the Pinkertons were checking trucks through. "Mine's Swan. X-u-a-n. You say it—'Swan.'" He slipped a newspaper clipping into my hand and stood up.

We went back to work.

The newspaper clipping was about chemical waste, and Cecil had printed "*In the U. S. of A.?*" on it. Traces of waste had shown up in the free milk given to schoolchildren. It dawned on me slowly—but even the most practical of men is subject to light. I asked Johnson, "What's in the canisters?"

"I don't know," he said.

I asked one of the drivers, working the question in gently behind some of my barber talk. "You taking this load to Binghamton?" I said.

"Nope," he said.

"Where, then?"

He gave me a nasty look. "None of your fucking business," he said.

That evening I waited around by the time clock for Andy, to ask him about the canisters. "Hey, Andy," I said.

"Kid," Andy said. He slid his card into the clock—*thunk*. "Listen, Kid," Andy said. "I've been wanting a word with you. Got a minute?"

"Sure," I said. "Buy you a beer down at the Old Pro, if you're game."

He looked around. "Nah. Another time." We walked out into the parking lot. "Listen, Kid. This Cecil? I know Frank asked you to look out for him. We all know that."

"He's okay, Andy," I said.

"Lemme finish. Maybe you ought to think about staying away from him a bit more. Let him go his own way."

"Why?" I said. I knew why, but I had an answer.

"He's one of them, Kid," Andy said.

"He was in Vietnam," I said. "Like Johnson was in the navy. Cecil was in Vietnam."

Andy shook his head, slowly, amused at me. "Johnson was on our side, Kid." He punched me on the shoulder in a friendly, buck-up way. "A gook's a gook, Kid. No two ways about it."

Somebody must have talked to Cecil, too, because he started staying away from me at lunch. He did keep passing me clippings, and I was pretty sure that Syrachem was one of the companies dumping chemical waste—some radioactive, some not—illegally. Pretty soon I found myself back with the boys at lunchtime. Things seemed normal again. Cecil ate and drank alone. He began to bring the smaller thermos again.

Let me tell you about ideals. They're like dandelions, easy to cut back but hard to kill. You may think you've given yours up and managed to become a normal member of society, one of the boys. But since you're a living, breathing human being, I warn you, they're there and they can get you.

Maybe there's another way to look at ideals. Mark Twain once said that the only reason he could see to quit tobacco was the sheer pleasure of taking it up again. Ideals might be the same as Twain's tobacco.

Or alcohol.

I began to drink a lot, then. I tried to talk to Cecil, but he shunned me. Not hurt. He just stayed away. All right, I thought, if that's the way you want it.

Then one night he came by the house. He brought me a jug of home-made rice wine. "To show I understand," he said. "No hard feelings?"

Ah, shit.

I drank a good bit of the stuff that night. I didn't sleep so easily.

I could hear Andy clearly the next morning, though. I was driving my pallet lift when I heard Andy shout, "Hummingbird!" He started weaving through the stacks like a drunk, demanding to know who had left the note on his cart. He wanted to ask Cecil, I could see that, but he didn't. He came to me. Was it true? he wanted to know.

It was.

I was a red nig?

I was.

Why had I lied to them all?

I hadn't. Isn't that something? I'd never even thought about it.

Toward lunchtime I was whipping along the dock, weaving slightly for the fun of it. Johnson came out.

"You should be more careful," Johnson said.

"Why, navy man?" I said. I regretted that. It stung him. Hell, he was only trying to live in this world like everyone else.

"You break one of them and we're all dead men," he said.

"Tell me, Johnson," I said. "Would that matter? Would it really matter? After the hostages are home, Sugar Ray's been walloped, and Dippy's slumped to .326?"

".296," he said. "Still slumping." I was let go, of course. I wasn't fired, just laid off. Syrachem didn't want me to call attention to them.

I went home and took up my ideals again, and felt richer for it, in a way. My father was disappointed. My insurance had lapsed. What can you do? Besides, I've figured it out that I have more money now, without insurance. And so what if I go to my grave with cavities?

I thought about trying to stir up trouble for Syrachem's dumping poison near Syracuse. But while I was deciding that no one except some guy named Xuan would care, Syrachem packed up and vanished. Poof! Gone. I wondered what became of Stuart, Andy, Henry Frank? Were they poor now, too?

Cecil came by, wearing a chauffeur's uniform. He works for a rich man now, named Khuri, which according to Cecil is the Arab equivalent to our Smith. Cecil wanted to tell me that he had not been the one who left the note with my last name on Andy's cart.

"I know," I said.

"You believe me?"

"Yes," I said. "And may you never have Westmoreland's Revenge again." I smiled. I still feel lighthearted in a way, but I feel older. I said that I felt as old as my grandfather. I feel older even, now—as ancient as my race itself.

Now I think: Mark Twain didn't have life insurance. I wonder if Dewey did?

They're dead, too, you know.

Toothpaste

I'VE BEEN TRYING TO FORGET HIM, BUT I THINK OF HIM ABOUT AS OFTEN as I brush my teeth.

Call me Addie or Delia. My name's not important. What I want to tell you about is this Indian man I met at a party, not long after my spouse equivalent and I had split up. I call him my spouse equivalent because, except for the legalities which I don't believe in, he was in most respects the equivalent of a husband—as Jacquie says, as long as you are willing to accept thirty seconds of limpness as some sort of equivalence. But that's not nice. I probably shouldn't say that. Like most men, he just had trouble making up his mind about what he wanted.

Anyway, I spent a long time by myself after he walked out, and I can't say I wasn't happy. But then Jacquie decided to have this party. She browbeat me until I agreed to show up.

"You have got to get out and around," she said. "Meet people. Otherwise, you're going to end up alone forever. You'll be sorry for that."

Would I? Even at the time, I wondered if I would have been sorry. After five years with a man who couldn't make up his mind about what love was, would I have been sorry to be alone and untroubled? Wasn't I content to live alone and simply do my work?

Looking back, I can see that I should have realized that the way I asked the question told me the answer: A woman can learn to live alone. But after a certain point, can anyone live untroubled?

So anyway, I bought a dress and went to Jacquie's party. As I stood awkwardly, chatting to some intensely Jewish fellow from the Upper West Side, I was overcome by the smell of coffee roasting in a nearby factory.

"I'd forgotten that," I said.

"Huh?" the fellow said.

I realized he had been talking to me seriously about Begin and Sharon. Israel. You know, interrelating the way serious people do at these parties. I tried to be smooth.

"I'm sorry," I said. "I was remembering how you can tell where you are in Lower Manhattan by the smell."

It's true: On one block, it's the smell of coffee. On another, the smell of chocolate or cheese. And if you happen to stumble into the letters— A, B, C, or D Avenue—it's the sour smell of garbage and despair.

"I'd forgotten," I said.

He wandered away.

Before long, I began to feel a bit out of place. Everyone looked staged with self-conscious gestures and ideas meant to please some invisible director in the production of life. Staged, or married—and that was the last thing I wanted to be around, happy married couples who call each other "Doodums" or "Honeybunch" or, worse, "Mommy."

There were chairs at the far end of the loft and I drifted toward them. I figured I could sit on one of them for an hour and then thank Jacquie and grab a cab home. That's when I ran into this Indian. I hadn't seen him at first, hiding there like an animal in its den, and by the time I had, it was too late.

The first thing he said to me, he said, "I've gotten a lot of bad press over the last year."

Certainly a curious way to open a conversation. I probably should have ended it there and gone back to my serious Jewish fellow. Or left. I didn't. As long as I had made the trip in from Brooklyn, I figured I might as well stick it out. Besides, he was kind of cute, kind of handsome. Both, you see, at the same time. He was one of those men who is born cute and ages so well that at thirty-five he is just starting to become handsome. What with his dark, smooth skin, you can see that he's the kind of man who, if he lives, will grow more handsome with the years. As a photographer who's been around, I can tell.

"I'm trying to avoid it," he said. His voice was monotone, like the chant of a note from way underground.

I decided to take a chance. "You're kind of cute," I said.

Most men would have blushed. He didn't. All he said was, "By default, I suppose."

"What do you mean?"

That's when he smiled for the first time, if you could call it a smile. It was brief, fleeting, like an involuntary twitch of the muscles. It reminded me of a time I was into shooting mad people. There was this one man in Central Park who grinned as he ate. He would take a bite of his sandwich and chew slowly, thoughtfully; all of a sudden, in mid-mastication, he would stop and grin to himself as though the secret of food had just been revealed to him. As I watched him, I could imagine how the grin had once, a long while ago, started as an attempt to disguise the utter loneliness that came from eating alone, and I could see how that affected grin had gradually become the madness of reality.

That's how this guy smiled as he said, "Look at them. Artists. They've come to New York to be artists. Like New York can give them talent. You have to admit," he said, before I could object, "some of them are quite unlike anyone you've ever dreamed, or would even want to dream."

"Some of them are interesting." I didn't really believe it myself, but it seemed the thing to say.

"Like that little serious fellow you were talking to before?" He laughed as gaily as a child. "He's so dull he'd wear Saran Wrap to a costume party."

He had me there. He was right. I laughed, too, almost happily—partly because he had noticed me earlier, which made me feel complimented, partly because his directness was so real.

"They're like Unitarians," he said. "They all believe in something higher called Art, but they've never met Art himself. You know why they keep coming to these parties?"

I shook my head.

"They want to check up on each other. Be sure that someone else hasn't stumbled onto Art, somehow. They all like each other because each one feels secretly that what he does is better than what anyone else does."

"I can see why you get bad press," I said. If I had felt out of place before, I suddenly felt as though I had stumbled onto Avenue D.

His smile vanished; he looked hurt. Hurting someone has always made me feel connected to him, and I didn't want to feel connected to anyone, not like that, so I told him, "I think I'm going to try the food."

"Go ahead," he said.

LATER, I HAD SOMEHOW BEEN ROPED INTO DANCING WITH THE LITTLE serious fellow. He danced as though he'd been practicing in front of a mirror—without success—and I was wondering where my friend with the bad press was, when the song ended.

"How was the food?" I heard him say. He was standing right behind me.

"That cobbler is terrible," I whispered, afraid that the person who had brought it was nearby.

He nodded, grinning that grin of his. "The woman who brought that? I've been to her house for dinner. Her food always looks like it came straight off the pages of *Good Housekeeping*. Tastes like it, too," he said loudly.

"Sssh," I said.

He looked confused.

"She might be listening," I said.

"So? It's *true,* isn't it?"

He waited until he could see that I understood that he didn't care who heard him, as long as what he said could be called true.

"You know, she can have three dinner parties off the food prepared for one. She freezes the untouched food and serves it the next time. Of course, eventually the dishes lose their shape and she has to throw them all out. Sometimes, I wonder if she makes it tasteless on purpose." He laughed and took a big slug of his drink. A drop or two dribbled down his chin.

The music started back up, and my partner touched me on the shoulder.

"I'm already taken," I said. "I'm going to dance with . . . what is your name, anyway?" I asked my friend with the bad press.

"Go ahead. I don't want to dance," he said.

I looked at him pleadingly. "Please," I said. He shook his head and laughed. The shit. I started to dance with the serious fellow, staying close to Bad Press, close enough to talk to him. "What is your name?"

He thought for a moment. "Why don't you call me Bert," he said, grinning his grin.

He didn't look like a Bert.

"Is that your name?"

"It will do," he said. "As my grandfather said, to see is to forget the name of what one sees. Call me anything you like." He gave my partner the once-over and moved away. He was impossible!

When the song ended, I found him again, back at the end of the loft, his eyes closed. He didn't look at me, but he must have heard me come up. "Coffee," he said. "Smells nice, doesn't it?" He was holding a bottle of Jack Daniels by the neck. He handed it to me. "Here," he said. "It'll help you forget."

I literally could feel the approach of my former partner. I panicked. "Please dance with me. Otherwise I'll have to dance with him," I said.

"You'd regret it. Dancing with me—you'll regret it," he said. "You'll see what happens, you dance with me."

"Please?" I begged, tugging at his arm.

"Oh, all right. Don't say I didn't warn you."

We danced. At first, Bert—or whatever his name was, since I was not convinced that was his real name—danced like the floor was hot, raising his right foot high, then his left foot high, doubling toward each knee as he raised it. You could see the music start to take over, and with each song he moved a little faster, until finally his eyes were closed and he was moving all over the floor. I wouldn't call him a good dancer, but the way the music seemed to fill him up was sort of sexy. I was enjoying myself, glad that Jacquie had browbeaten me into coming.

Suddenly, he stopped and planted his feet again. His lips were clenched, like he was pouting. "What's wrong?" I said.

"You hear that?" he said. "It's happening."

"Hear what?"

He grinned, but bitterly. "I knew this Navajo woman, once," he said. "She could listen to radio music and sort out German codes hidden beneath the static and the Mozart. I'm like that with conversations. There's someone over there betting on us."

I looked around to see what he meant.

"See the fat one over there? She says I'm a prick. She's giving odds on whether or not I'm going to go home with you tonight." As if that wasn't clear enough, he added, "Her odds are that I'm going to fuck you. How's that make you feel?"

"Ignore them," I said. I was embarrassed, but the idea of his going home with me, well. . . .

"I wouldn't sleep with him," I heard someone say.

Before I realized it Bert had stopped dancing and was standing there, clenching his fists as though trying to hold himself back. He walked over to the woman and said, "If I had wanted to fuck the Pillsbury Doughboy, I would have been a baker."

It was cruel, and yet I felt the justice of it. The woman staggered over toward the food where she stood with large eyes staring at everyone, stuffing cocktail wienies into her mouth. Not wanting to laugh in front of her, I dashed into the bathroom.

I FOUND HIM OUT ON THE FIRE ESCAPE, DRINKING STRAIGHT FROM THE bottle. I stuck my head out. "Bert?"

"Go away."

I climbed out onto the metal grid. A damp breeze was blowing off the river, unblocked by the West Side Highway. It felt good. "Come back inside," I said. "Please, Bert?"

"Call me Al," he said.

"Al. Bert. I don't care what your name is," I said.

He seemed impressed by my saying that. It triggered something. "I didn't want to do that," he said. "Try to understand. Try to see that at some point the image of Poppin' Fresh takes over. I hate Poppin' Fresh. All pudgy and pale. I hate that woman talking about me like I'm some kind of rabbit."

I touched his cheek. I tried to be sympathetic. "How does a rabbit screw a water buffalo, anyway," I said. It was lame.

"I don't want to be an asshole," he said. "It's been this way since my wife and I . . . she used to come to these with me. She kept me under control. Jeez, I miss her sometimes. No," he said. "No, that's a lie. I miss her all the time; it's just when things like that happen that I notice how much I miss her. She was one of the nicest people I knew. Besides," he said, smiling that smile of his, "she liked me."

I tried to concentrate on the smell of coffee. I didn't need to talk about girlfriends or boyfriends, wives and husbands. People who have never split up don't know the truth about how we who have can feel. It's not that we miss our spouse equivalents in the way of wanting them back. No, it's more that being used to their habits of speech and move-ment, the old habits get in the way of making new adjustments. I know: I have been attracted to a man and the unexpected thought of some lit-tle thing my spouse equivalent did will suddenly take the air out of my tires.

"She left me," he said, even though I hadn't asked. "Guess it got to be too hard being married to an Indian who collected bad press. People used to think she was a bit strange, too, marrying someone like me. Sort of like Bear calling Crow black, isn't it?"

He turned toward me. In the light from inside, his eyes looked like an old terrier's with cataracts. "Don't look so sad," he said. "I don't blame her for leaving. It's just that now I have to take the bad press all by myself. That's hard. It's wearing me away. No one," he said, "will ever love me like that again."

I didn't know what to do. As dispirited as he seemed, I liked him. He was different, if nothing else. I moved to him and put my arms around him, leaning my head against his chest. I could hear his heart; if I never remember another thing about him, I'll always remember the way that heart sounded. Deep. Slow, when it should have been racing.

"Maybe," I said. "Maybe someone will."

Standing there in the cool breeze, the silence outside competing with the noise within, he held me. Then he pushed me away, holding my shoulders at arm's length.

"This always happens, now. People placing bets on me. I'm not a fucking rabbit, not some kind of stud horse you can place bets on." He began to laugh a laugh that had the same mad reality of his grin. "Once," he said, "I was at this party out on Staten Island. This woman with a face smiling like a Matachina mask is raising my odds. When she gets to ten-to-one, I am dizzy with self-hatred. I can't take the fluorescent lights of the room we are standing in, so I escape to the bathroom."

He extracted a hand-rolled cigarette, lit it, and offered it to me. "You know what I did?" he said, letting the smoke drift out from his nose.

"Obviously not."

"I didn't really think about it until the husband told his fourteen-year-old daughter to go to bed and her mother said, 'And be sure to brush your teeth.' I started to stop the daughter, and then I figured what the hell, let her get a taste of what life is going to be like."

"You were in the bathroom?" I said.

"Not by that time. But I had spent some time in there. First thing I'd done is smash the glass from the hand mirror and stand there look-ing through the oval frame into the wall mirror over the sink. Considering how a stud bull should look. Figuring I'd fix any stud action for the night, I took a Dexamil. Then I masturbated into a plastic cup in the toothbrush holder. Twice. Between times, I smoked a number laced with cocaine and thought about my wife. As fucked up as I was after that, there was no way I was going to climb into the rack with anyone that night."

I was reeling a bit, but he had grasped my shoulders again. "What did you do when the little girl was told to brush her teeth?"

"I grabbed someone and started to dance like we were going to war. With some woman who proceeded to explain carefully to me how I was so selfish that she doubted I'd be good in bed. Isn't it funny how with white women everything comes down to a question of what you should do for them? They're all afraid of real sex and anyone who isn't is selfish."

"Are you?" I said.

"What?"

"Selfish."

"Sure I am," he said. "Aren't you?" I shrugged. "If I am, though, it's only because I'm trying to keep a tiny bit of myself alive and distinct from all this democracy of nice and plain. I guess no matter what I do, I'll be an asshole. And now, because of the bad press I get, everyone has predetermined that I will be an asshole."

"Why do you go, then?" It didn't make sense to me.

"Because people convince me that unless I get out and around, I'll end up alone. At least at first that was why. I have also used the excuse that if you drink alone, you're an alcoholic and everybody knows about drunken Indians, eh? Now, it's like I've lost my soul. My personality. I've played the role so long that the role seems to be all I have left."

Oh, Al, I wanted to say. You don't have to be like this. I should have; I didn't.

He blew out another hit. "I must need them as much as they need me. I've become the age and ugliness that's inside each of them. Like a smashed hand mirror, they can look at themselves through me." He was not laughing when he said, "Wonderful, isn't it? I have a purpose in life. Most people don't have that. The funny part is that ever since that party on Staten Island, the fourteen-year-old has had a crush on me."

"So what are you going to do?" I said, thinking about the fourteen-year-old.

"Do?" he said.

"About the parties. The bad press."

"They've made me. Just like Geronimo, they've got to live with me, don't they? Next week or the week after, there'll be another party. I'll take a Dexamil and say mean things or do something to offend someone. Feelings will be felt. People will take a look at themselves, not like what they see, and call me an asshole. I'll be a stud horse. The dancing rabbit. I can't help myself." He added brightly, before he ducked back inside the loft, "I'll be there. You can bet on that."

HOW LONG I STAYED ON THE FIRE ESCAPE LISTENING TO THE WIND AND trying to sort out what it was I was feeling, I don't remember. I watched a helicopter beat its way toward the World Trade Center; before long it, or another helicopter, beat back out over the river and disappeared toward the foreignness of Jersey.

I wanted to work: I didn't need this Indian who called himself Bert or Al. I had only recently begun to feel free of the burden of memories my spouse equivalent had not taken with him when he left. I knew that I had lost ground because of him to the younger artists inside. Lost double ground, because the younger ones seemed to have no sense of good or bad. They cranked out piece after piece, and there was always someone willing to give a show to the constant line of production, as long as the line didn't change. The last thing I needed, then, was involvement with a man who would extract time and energy the way I knew he would.

By the time I climbed back through the window, he was at the door looking sheepish and not a little resentful as he had words with Jacquie. I made the first decision then, and asked him if I couldn't call him sometime.

"If you want," he said. He wrote down a number. "Here. Ask for Al. I'll know who it is."

"I'll call," I said. I touched his elbow. He left.

When the door closed behind him, I was left standing beside Jacquie. "He can be such an asshole sometimes," she said, and I heard another door closing with the thud of a heartbeat, this one between me and Jacquie, between me and the people I had been used to calling my friends. There was no use protesting. We saw such different things.

Instead I made a second decision and, grabbing my jacket, rushed out after him to ask him to come home with me, even though I suspected that because of the betting that had gone on, he wouldn't—or couldn't. I thought I caught a glimpse of him heading toward Canal Street, but when I reached the corner he had vanished into thin air. Wandering around looking for him, I came across a wino and a junkie, nodding together in mutual need against a wind that had grown colder. Staring at them, I wasn't frightened. Rather, I felt an odd kind of hope. I imagined that suffering of all kinds could overcome the separation each of us feels almost daily. A scream that sounded like silk tearing brought me to my senses, made me aware of where it was I had gotten to, and I ran back to Jacquie's to phone a cab.

That night when I went to brush my teeth, I nearly gagged. I decided that dental hygiene could wait and I went and did what I've been doing a lot of since that party—I stared out my front window. Across the street, some of my black neighbors were having a party at full volume. A couple emerged into the streetlight and headed away; a woman leaned out the door and shouted, "Y'all coming back?" and the man answered that they were.

Back? I thought. It was 3 A.M. I knew what the pair was going off to do. I recognized in the man's husky voice their purpose. I grinned to myself. Where white people seem really mad, black people seem only mad with reality. That party went on all night and well into Sunday, and the noise which kept me awake made me feel as lonely as I have ever felt with or without my spouse equivalent.

So the next day, I called the number Al had given me. A man's voice answered, and laughed when I asked for Al.

"No one here by that name," he said.

I repeated the number I had dialed, and still he laughed. "That's my number," he said. "Never heard of Al."

Since then, I have gone to every party, hoping to see him there, and at each one I have found myself asking more often why these people even get up in the morning. And yes, thinking about what Al would say, I have found myself speaking more and more directly. I say things, or I sit in a corner and wait and watch until I am sure he—I wish I knew his real name—isn't going to show up. Then I call a cab or wander down to the nearest subway.

At the last party, I overheard someone mutter the word "Bitch!" and I knew she was speaking about me. About me!

I admit that I smiled as though I had a secret.

And I did.

You see, the strange thing was this: In her mind, it was true; the fact that it was in her mind argued that I didn't have to care.

Rosa

WHAT HE WANT TO COME ROUND HERE FOR, ASKING HIS CRAZY QUES-
tions 'bout how you do this or that or 'bout how you feel. What's it to
him how I feel, anyhow? It don't make a bit of difference. He write it
all down in that tiny book of his and say, Hmmm, and then hold the
book away from his eyeballs and make his eyes narrow and say, Hmmm,
again, like the second "Hmmm" going to change what the first one
mean.

Elvira, she comes in without knocking. Ain't no use to knock anyways since it seems like everybody here is here. They playing cards, but
they won't let me watch 'cause of luck. I'm with child and that's bad for
luck before the fields are done. Anyway, Vira come bursting in and
stood, looking.

Careful, Vira, Hugh calls. Whoa, there. You'll rip our red tag. All
the men laugh.

The boy say the red tag means that the house ain't fit to live in. He told this to the men, but Hugh says, I suppose that means the man's beer ain't fit to drink neither. Hugh likes that, hot days, when the foreman trucks beer into the field for them.

And our pee ain't fit for the ground, one of the other men says.

They make fun of the poor boy, but I can tell he means good and I feel kind of sorry for him. Usually they come in wearing high-color pants that fits them like a sack of beans, but he's wearing clothes like the rest of the men here. He's skinny, like a beanpole, too. He stand there shifting from foot to foot like a lost dog, lost, with his tail cut off and showing no wag like Yaller.

I called the dog Yaller 'cause I heard of a movie dog called that and 'cause that's what he did, yalled. He didn't bark, rightly, but sort of set back and opened his teeth and hollered at you and only stopped if you did the same. He was a bother, sometime, but he was funny, too. Like when he used to chase old Beanie round and round his truck.

Beanie was the foreman before Mister Mister (make him wild, we call him that), a big buck Indian, and Yaller didn't like his proud ways and you let Beanie raise his voice just once and Yaller would set back and raise his and then commence chasing Beanie till one or the other was peaked and couldn't move. If it was Beanie quit first, Yaller would chomp on his ankle, mostly for show.

One day Beanie let Yaller have both barrels of his gun. I sort of missed old Yaller. You get used to missing if you've grown up here like I have. Ain't nothing last. Missed Beanie too when he was put off the job, being both his legs badly broke soon thereafter.

So here comes this man, no more'n a boy, really, 'minding me of Yaller. He's trying to tell the men they can get better, people don't live like this no more, and Hugh just say, You mean we ain't living? The men laugh and go on playing cards and the boy stands there by the door till he sees me in the corner and sort of nudges over to me.

Mind if I sit? he says.

Go 'head, I say, and he sits on the floor with his knees pulled up.

Chair over there, I say.

This is fine, thank you, he says, and I think, Thank you, for what? Makes me know he means good. Nobody's ever said thank you to me at all that I can mind, and he says it just for the saying.

Don't pay them no mind, I say, feeling like the boy could use it.

He looks at me and grins. I never in my life seen a mouthful like that afore, white as the day they was put in his head by the Lord, and I'm thinking, Lord, Lord, what's he done so bad you send him here?

That's when he begins asking and writing. Things like how many rooms we got in the house and I say, You're sitting in half of them, and how many people live in the house, and what kind of toilet we use and I say, The one the good Lord above gave us.

He writes and writes and says, Hmmm, now and then.

That's when Elvira come in, and I know why she's there 'cause she's heard, and there's nothing she likes better than to get holt on a different man. While she standing at the door joking with the men, I warn this boy to give her lots of room, lots of room, you hear, 'cause her husband Packy there cut you to pieces for no reason. It was Packy who broke both Beanie's legs, I'm certain.

The boy looks scared and I'm glad, 'cause it's true and Vira's not much more'n a whore to tell right.

What you want, Elvira, I say.

Hey, Rosa, Vira say to me. I come to borrow your thing. You know, the thing I borrowed last year. For lemons and things. It gets the juice better than mine. Can I?

I believe she wants to borrow your lemon juicer, the boy says.

Juicer, Vira laughs. Juicer. You hear that, he say it's called a juicer. The boy just turns red. Don't you worry, honey, Elvira says when she stops laughing. We only fooling.

Say, you're kind of cute, she says, and reaches out to touch him. His eyes get wide and he leans away from her like her hand's a knife.

He tries to go on with his questions, holding his book up between

him and Elvira like she's the Devil himself and the book will safen him.
He seems kind of surprised when he asks about relieving yourself in the
fields and I say, Depends.

On what? he says.

Whether the boss is there or not.

What do you mean?

If he ain't there, you just go right where you at. Other way, you got
to waste time by going all the way out to them outhouses they truck in
to the edge of the field.

You mean people go to the bathroom right on the crop? he says. I
nod. We're paid by the piece, anyways. The boy don't write that down,
I see.

Do you think I could go out to the field with you? he says. He's sounding tired. Wonder how he'd do, picking. Have to fatten him up some.

I'd like to, I say, and this is true. I miss the other people when they
out there working, and I got to stay by myself in here. Get scared sometimes. Lonesomely.

Hey, Hugh, Elvira call. You hear? Rosa want to go out into the
beans.

Hugh don't even look up. He's playing cards and when he's got a
hand, ain't nothing to change his face.

Elvira grins at me. Rosa can't, she tells the boy.

The boy looks up at me. Can't he see I'm with child? Last time a
woman with child went 'mong the beans rain come along and washed
all the vines down. I'd like to oblige him. But Hugh would whip me, if
I took the chance.

The boy looks at Elvira the same way he looks at me. She can't,
Elvira says. She's pregnant and they's things in the fields, things
that crawl up her dress and try to hurt her baby if she did. Else if they
couldn't, they waste the crop 'cause they angry.

It look like the boy just been kneed in the pants by Vira. He look
back to me and say, Do you believe that?

What else? I say. It's true, ain't it?

He lets his head hang between his knees and his book drop at the floor. From the men, I can hear that Hugh has won a big hand and that's good 'cause we'll need the money. I don't say anything to spoil his luck, though he mostly wins. I'll miss Hugh. After tomorrow, the men will move on to Florida in the truck and I won't see him till the spring when he come north again.

The boy finally gets round to going. Well, he says, well, thanks for your time. Elvira just look away. She's sad to see him go soon like this.

You come back and see us again any old time, I say, and smile.

He just nods and tries to smile back. He knows like me he won't never be back. Next year like the last, another one younger than him will come with the same questions, get the same answers, but it won't be him. Seems like they been doing that forever, and one of these days I going to commence wondering why and not stop until I've got it figured.

Vira and I grin at one another. She know, too. Maybe she can figure it with me. Till then, we know even we got a hundred red tags we still be living here.

Neither

"ARE YOU HANUKKAH OR CHRISTMAS?" HE HAD ASKED HER, DEADLY serious and inquisitive, as if it were a question that mattered very much.

"I'm neither," she had replied, and at first he'd looked confused as if she'd abandoned him somehow with her answer, as if he were chewing her answer and the taste was unfamiliar to his palate.

Anna realized how thick her accent was still, even after all these years, as though the tongue remembered things the mind did not. His face had surprised her, blank almost, without emotion, as he'd pointed at the house behind hers and said, "They are Christmas."

She, Anna Ruktashel, was not a sentimental person. Indeed not. Sentiment had been torn from her when she had escaped her homeland with her brothers. She had no patience with it; it was a weakness and it could kill you if you let it. So the boy's peculiar use of *they* had not struck her until, months later, she had seen him fall in the gutter beside his house and lie there as though paralyzed by something. But she had known that was his house he had pointed to since she had watched him before, solemnly playing by himself in the small dirt lot behind his house, which was fenced off from the rest of the backyard.

She had been drawn to her window by the bark of her old dog, whose run ran parallel to the dirt lot. The boy was lining up several of his toy trucks—earthmovers, dump trucks, and the like—making their formation exact as if they were about to embark on an important task, much the way her own father had lined up his serfs to explain how their lives had changed.

The boy had marched over to the fence near the dog, said something, and stuck his hand through the chain-links to rub its muzzle. She had started for the door, afraid the dog might bite. She'd stopped when the dog lay down quiet, and watched.

The boy had wheeled, gone inside his house, and quickly returned carrying a round cylinder that looked like a coffee tin with a bright blue cloth tied over the open end. He seemed to search for the right spot, and then he set the tin down lengthwise, placing two stones on either side to keep it from rolling off the mound he had selected.

One by one the trucks were mobilized, and the noise he made starting their engines caused the shepherd's ears to point and then relax. Anna watched the child as the earthmover cleared and leveled a large patch of ground. By the time she had finished lunch, the yellow truck with the scoop on the front (what were those called?) was digging a rectangular hole out of the cleared space. What fascinated Anna was the patience, the precision. When the boy's mother had come out to the fence and spoken to him, he backed the scoop truck out of the hole and lifted its shovel before he turned to her to answer. Even though he was a chubby child, there seemed to be something like noblesse expressed by his manner, by the way he stood and spoke to his mother. And it made Anna remember. Later, when Anna had pulled her two-wheeled basket back from the corner market, the trucks were gone, and the mound where the tin had been was marked by a makeshift little cross, which was gone the next morning, blown or carried away. It was never replaced.

"ANNA?"

Anna sat in a high-backed chair, tense, and listened. For her, the dark house, lit only by the gray filtered light that sneaked in around the blinds, had become a cave in which the voice echoed, gradually dying out after several seconds—minutes even. She could not hear any movement on the porch. He was standing there, endlessly patient, waiting for her to open the door she no longer could. She imagined him there, and she realized that after only three days, she could not imagine his face, which had become liquid in her mind like her memory of her childhood, of Russia, of the house she forced herself to believe had looked like the magazine pictures he had brought to her. It was a face that was neither young nor old, neither light nor dark, neither . . . anything at all. It was that, partly, which made her close her doors to him.

The voice called out again and was followed by the rapping of knuckles against her front door. Again the echo, which seemed to center in herself, as if she were the heart or soul of the clapboard house. Go away, she thought. Go away, child. No, that was not right. Imp. Imp, that was what the boy was, sneaking into her house, bringing with him his solitude, his unexpressed loneliness. You made it happen, Anna. You were the one who said "Hello, Christmas" to him as he stood watching, outside the fence. She remembered.

"I'm not Christmas," he had corrected, "they are." Again he had pointed.

The way he spoke bothered her. She had not understood why until the day he had said, "We are friends, aren't we."

It was not a question, and she had frozen in her movements for a second and looked at him in horror. Friends? He was looking at her. He had said it to the air around, noting a fact, like planting a little cross on a grave he had so carefully prepared.

They, they, they. He, or she. Never Mama, Papa. Never a name attached, never a gap, as if the Bosporus had closed up long ago, and this little child were its own lake, its own sea.

The horror had passed as she became used to his serious manner. He reminded her of her brother who was dead, of how her older brother had taught her and her younger brother to believe only in themselves as they had moved like nomads from place to place across Europe and into America. She had begun to call the boy a little pecheneg, a noble savage, a name which he had liked and used as he insisted on her repeating a particular story of Russia. He always said, "Pecheneg wants to know why you fled Russia," or "Tell Pecheneg about the piano." Anna had played for him what she remembered of the pieces which were scattered like ashes, pieces such as the Kreuzer Sonata, the boy's favorite.

Anna had even begun to draw strength from this savage little count. He was the youngest of three children, and things seemed to affect him so slightly that it gave her a kind of hope. Once, even, she found herself reaching out to touch him on the top of his head, as she had seen his sister do one morning as the pair crossed the boulevard to school. She had stopped herself, frightened by the awareness that this pecheneg could be snatched from her. Or was it something else that had made her stop?

"Anna? It's Pecheneg. American Russian." He said "Roo-shun," imitating her heavy accent. Was he mocking her? No. He was too young for that. Still, she'd had the feeling he was making fun of her, even accusing her, at other times, as when she'd been telling him about how her elder brother would have been a count had the tsar not been overthrown, how she would have been a noblewoman herself, except for the flight from Russia. The boy had had a strange look in his eye that seemed to say, "Would have been, but you aren't."

Anna crept over to the mantel, where she grasped the glass dome of the brass clock and stared into it. She was afraid, this time, for she knew that some horrid part of herself wanted to open the door and let him see her face, how it had changed since just four days ago. She gripped the dome more tightly, tempted to try to squeeze it between her fingers until it shattered. What could she do? He would understand neither the way she looked nor the closed door. So what were her choices? If she could wait long enough, he would give up and go home, go somewhere else and leave her alone. She was too old for the struggle that went on each time his voice echoed through the door and into her house.

She sank onto the piano stool and began to run her fingers over the walnut of the keyboard cover. She closed her eyes.

All the images of her life had become liquid like music except for one, and it was one she had not known she remembered. She saw the face of her younger brother bob to the surface of the river, his mouth open but muffled by the rushing water that swept him away from her beneath the mist of an early dawn. She had been carrying him; she had slipped; and she had hung there, watching, rooted in place, hesitant. In the terror of their continued flight, she had convinced herself that her older brother had pulled her up onto the shore she clung to, carefully convincing herself that she had had no choice. There had been, after all, no time for pain.

Anna had never questioned what she had felt, never questioned the seconds of hesitation until now, and it occurred to her that a part of her faltering might have been resentment. This she put out of her mind.

It was the boy's fault that this was happening to her. His weakness had caused it. She had seen the noble little figure marching alone, in the midst of a group of children, out of the schoolyard across the street. Frightened, she had been staring out the window at the November storm that poured water onto the automobiles that pulled blindly up along the curbs, accepted children, and lumbered away. The gutters ran so full that only the centerline of the boulevard was not three inches deep in swirling brown water that rushed violently toward the riverbed into which the streets drained. She saw her pecheneg pause, snapping his arms out for balance, and step into the gutter on the far side. She saw the water snatching at the folds in his oversized rubber boots. His steps became quicker, braver, as he crossed the center. And then suddenly, next to the nearer curb, he slipped and fell, and the water tumbled him over, once, like a log in a flash flood.

He lay there.

"Get up," Anna whispered. Then she began to curse him, his weakness (this, too, she could see herself doing behind her closed eyes). Still he lay there, paralyzed, as Anna waited and watched for someone to help him. Riveted to the window, she was barely able to move her head and glance up the street for an approaching car. No one seemed to notice he was there. She saw his hand stretch out slowly, burdened by the neoprene of his slicker, the fingers grabbing at the edge of the curb. Why didn't he just get up? The fingers caught hold and he began to drag his stiff body up, inch by inch, onto the curb, the other hand clutching at the small tree in the middle of the grass strip between the sidewalk and curb. Both hands, now. Anna's lips began to move silently, quickly, praying, her own legs unresponsive as her blood beat out a fear she hated, a resentment she had forgotten she had ever known. She could feel her face tighten around a scream that did not make any sound, a scream that revealed itself in her face permanently, as though it had always been there, even after the boy sat on the sloshy grass, shaking as though sobbing, his face buried deep in his hands.

No, Anna thought, he was not a pecheneg. He was only a little boy who referred to his parents the same way a person of her class would have referred to the tsar, a boy whose connection with her was sentimental only and who had forced doors ajar that opened onto nothing. This, more than anything else, struck her. Since then, for three days, she had avoided looking into a mirror.

Anna looked around herself in the dimly lit room. There was nothing here but bric-a-brac. Everything seemed to have lost what identity it had had and, no longer her brother's, it was all her own.

Maybe she ought to pull the boy inside, let him look into her face, which she believed had hardened like molten rock around her fear.

Yes.

As she summoned the nerve to open the door, Anna heard the gate outside click shut and she knew the boy was marching stolidly home. She did not go to the window to peek out, but leaned back, her fingers resting on the keyboard panel. Nothing. She could feel the stains soaking into the furniture, and hear the threads in the carefully woven patterns of the upholstery begin to snap. She did not have to go to the window to see what she needed to see, and her fingers began to move as the Emperor Concerto began to sound chord by chord through her memory.

Cowboys and Indians

My mother, Alcie, didn't have to wheedle to get my father to agree that in order to integrate me into the world of work and necessity it was best for them to ignore the fact that I was part Indian. Albert adored Alcie, and on the night he proposed he was so nervous and so overcome with gratitude for her saying she would marry him as long as any children were raised American, he didn't even think to ask her what she meant. He was willing to agree to anything. He was that kind of guy, anyway, agreeable. At least that's what people said when he spent Thanksgiving Day cooking a turkey and Alcie spent the day and dinner criticizing him. "You're so agreeable, Albert," they would say. "One of the nicest guys you'll ever hope to meet," they'd say to each other while Albert was out of the room carving and Alcie had followed him into the kitchen to make sure he did it right.

Alcie's caution and Albert's willingness proved successful over the years. By the time I was ten, Alcie was vindicated for her vigilance when

Ashley Packard the Third extended me a formal invitation to his birthday party. Walking up beside me at school and surveying the playground like Waterloo, as though he owned both it and the smallish humans playing upon its field, he desultorily reached into his pocket and pulled out an envelope. It was smudged and curled at the corners. He looked at it, examining it carefully, turning it over and back as though he wasn't sure how it had gotten into his pocket, and then with a sigh handed it to me.

"Here," he said. "My mother wants me to give you this." Then he wheeled and walked away.

Weary as Alcie was from her day's work at Syntex, the birth control company, where she put into practice what she so firmly believed, as she was in the habit of saying, her joy at seeing my invitation was so infectious that I felt happy and hopeful. Her joy was so great that I merely ignored Albert later that night when, putting me to bed, he came into my room smelling like wildflowers and wine and asked gently if I really wanted to go spend a day with rich kids in the hills.

"If you don't want to go," he whispered, "just tell me."

"I want to go," I said, my residual joy and excitement hardly letting me wonder why Albert was asking.

The next morning when I came into the kitchen for my cereal, Albert was gone and Alcie was sitting alone at the breakfast table as chipper as chipper could be. The prospect of taking me shopping for just the right present for Ashley Packard made her loquacious.

THE DAY OF THE PARTY, ALCIE FOLLOWED THE DIRECTIONS MRS. Packard had given to her over the phone. We drove up into hills I had only seen from a distance. Alcie could not help but exclaim.

"My," she said, her breath caught short. "My, my. Would you look at that?"

She drove slowly, ducking to peek up through the windshield at the houses that towered over us on rises and hillsides, most of them behind gates with shrubs and grassy lawn enough to carpet the White House. Every intersection seemed to have a stop sign, and one block even had unpainted ridges of asphalt across the road that forced you to slow down before you drove over them. So Alcie had plenty of time to admire the way these people lived. There was every kind of tree, all of a size that made the cherry tree I had planted in our backyard seem insignificant. I squirmed at her envy and complained that my new linen slacks itched.

"Don't be silly," she said.

"It should be in the next block," I said, folding up the directions Alcie had printed out for me to read.

She pulled over to the side of the road. "You have your tie?"

In my pocket I had a clip-on bow tie, which I was instructed to put on if more than one other child was wearing a tie.

"Uh-huh," I replied.

"When may you not wear the tie?"

I sighed. "Less than two."

"And when must we put it on?"

"More than or equal to two," I said.

She nodded her head. A litany of behavior followed, but even that did not prepare me for Ashley Packard's home. Nothing would have. It was a sprawl of storied adobe with lacy ironwork on the upstairs balconies. A red tile roof, four chimneys, shrubs cut like diamonds or shaped like birds—ducks or dodoes, I thought, dodoes being my favorite—and an arched oak plank door, the planks held in line with black iron straps and bolts.

A man answered the door.

"Mr. Packard?" I said.

He did not reply. Instead, he held one finger up like a candle to light my way, turned, and led me down a long hall at the end of which he opened another door for me, behind which waited a small ancient lady.

"Mrs. Packard?" I asked.

"Edna," she replied. She smiled kindly and lifted the gift out of my hands and set it on a side table piled with other presents. My package looked mighty small beside the others. I wished I hadn't come. I followed Edna through large French doors that opened onto a slate veranda. "Endymion Hummingbird," she announced, and then she withdrew, closing the French doors as she went.

"Dym," I said, but she disappeared so quickly that I said it to myself. I preferred "Dym." Alcie had insisted on "Endymion" when I was born. I hated "Endymion" so much that I actually preferred the teasing and bullying that always went with "Dym" the first time other kids heard the name.

After what seemed like several minutes a woman in tennis whites rose from a circle of women sitting in the shade of a patio umbrella and strolled across the veranda to me. She reached out and shook my hand.

"You must be Endymion," she said. "Did your mother come in?" She straightened up and glanced around quickly as though she expected Alcie might be hiding in the topiary. "No? Well, that's a shame. That's unfortunate. I was so looking forward to meeting her. Another time perhaps."

"Ashley," she called. "Endymion has arrived."

"Dym," I said weakly.

Ashley ignored her. He had organized a game of croquet out on the expanse of lawn and he was busy telling the other children how to play.

Mrs. Packard gave me a gentle shove. "Perhaps you should go on and introduce yourself to the others," she said.

I already knew Elizabeth and Pinky from school. Elizabeth always made a big deal about her mother being with Amnesty International. She had dressed up by putting a rhinestone stud in her nostril. She refused to look at me. But Pinky, with her rosy cheeks and frilly dress, grinned and said "Hi" as if she were glad to see me. Her cheeks flushed, and she giggled. The children I didn't know included Patty, whose family was in publishing; Leland, whose family used to be in railroads and land speculation; and Mark, whose family did hotels. Edsel's family was obvious. Corliss's was in jewelry.

"Diamonds, in particular," Corliss added. She was darker than the rest, with black hair and the shadowy promise of a mustache when she reached adulthood. I was grateful for her. I was grateful because there was at least one other child there who did not look bathed in lanolin.

Leland decided to bug me about what my parents did. I didn't want to tell him. So he started going around telling everyone how we were probably on welfare. "His kind usually are, you know," he kept saying, laughing derisively.

I was rigid with anger and trying my best not to leap upon him and wrestle his puny little butt to the ground and sit on his chest and threaten him until he cried "uncle," when Mrs. Packard descended from the veranda to interrupt.

"What might be the problem?" she inquired, softly but firmly taking hold of the nape of my neck with her ring hand. Her grip tightened when Leland shouted that I was on welfare.

After a minute her grip relaxed, and as blood rushed back into my brain, she said, "Don't be silly, Leland. Of course Endymion's family is not on public assistance. Is it?" she asked, smiling down at me like a sergeant of the Sandanista army, her smile a mixture of knowing how I had better answer and a kind of indifferent cruelty.

I shook my head rapidly from side to side.

"Endymion's family does. . . ." Her smile vanished as she searched her memory for what the school had told her my mother and father did. "Endymion's family does . . . ," she repeated, this time making it plain that I was to fill in the blank.

Panicked, I tried to imitate her formality. "Pro-phy-lac-tics," I said, pronouncing each syllable distinctly, clearly, trying hard to keep my tongue from forking around the log of the word.

Mrs. Packard seemed to freeze. None of the children moved. Pinky giggled, holding her hand up to cover her mouth. Mrs. Packard's nails dug into my neck.

They didn't understand. They did not know what prophylactics were. They thought I was making fun of Mrs. Packard, imitating her formal tone while giving her a nonsensical answer. They thought I was insulting her.

"Rubbers," I blurted, trying to save the situation. "My mother makes rubbers so that people can. . . ."

"Yes. We know," Mrs. Packard said coldly. "Not public assistance, at the least." I thought she muttered, "Not much better, though" as she drew Ashley aside to talk to him.

I took over Ashley's mallet on the great expanse of the croquet court. I sensed that Mrs. Packard and Ashley were talking about me. I even caught one or two of their words as I followed my ball from wicket to wicket. Ashley kept shrugging his shoulders as Mrs. Packard waved her hand in a tight circle, like someone trying to get you to hurry up.

Pinky knocked her ball across the court. She came over and poked me in the ribs. "Stupid," she said. "You'll never get invited back if you say things like that."

"I didn't want to be invited in the first place," I whispered.

Pinky ignored me. She bent over to strike her ball and her stiff party dress rose above her buttocks to reveal panties with squares of abstract colors surrounded by words.

"Sssss," I hissed. "Someone's been scribbling on your panties."

She straightened up and smoothed her crinoline petticoat down. She looked me in the eye. "That's not scribbling," she answered haughtily. "That's art."

While Ashley and his mother argued, the croquet game quickly degenerated into a turnless, random striking of balls. Everyone but Patty began to laugh and have fun, chasing after their balls this way and that as they got knocked off the court. I struck Edsel's ball such a blow that it bounced and rolled until it ended up in a small stream at the bottom of the lawn. Corliss's ball went skipping across the tennis court. It spun and skipped on the cement and seemed to gather momentum before it vanished into the trees beyond. Corliss watched it disappear. Then she shrugged as if it were too much trouble to go after it.

After croquet came lunch, served to us on the veranda on lap trays gaily decorated with birthday crepe. Pinky could see my confusion and, feeling compassionate, she sat beside me, taking me under her wing, helping me figure out just what it was we were eating. I paid her close attention, repeating the names because Alcie would want to know. But after she told me that the black stuff I liked so much was caviar and Leland, jealous of Pinky's attentions to me, clarified that as fish eggs with little baby fish embryos inside which is what gave them their crunch, I decided that among such people it might be better to settle for not knowing. I could make up what I told Alcie. I concentrated on the color and texture and taste of the foods. But I no longer asked Pinky what they were—who could tell but there might be Ubangi brains in some innocent-looking bowl of stuff.

Some of the food, of course, like the melon and other fruit, I recognized. If Alcie asked—and she would—I would be expansive about the fruit, or tell her all about the ice cream and cake which was to be served, as Ashley kept promising, after games.

Even though none of the other kids would speak to me after Pinky got so mad because I asked politely if she'd let me see her panties again, as the afternoon wore on I began to wonder if it wouldn't be kind of nice to live like this. I felt torn, as though half of me thought it would, what with servants to deliver and remove food or brown-skinned men to trim the bushes and sweep the tennis court, and the other half just wanted to sweep the court with the silent men and go home to my own world at the end of the day. We played ring toss and lawn darts and hunted for small treasures hidden about the yard, during which I found Corliss's croquet ball. I felt happy. Contented. And after each game, each of us was handed a door prize by the man who had let me through the front door so that by the end we all had quite a stash.

The only thing that bothered me was that Ashley proved to be a master at cheating. He acted as though he did not have to follow the rules, and he thereby won all of the games. For example, the manservant brought out a large board with a donkey painted on it by a local artist (we were told); each of us gave pinning on its tail while blindfolded our best shot, for which we all received the biggest and best consolation prizes—even Leland, who missed the entire board. Ashley went last, of course, and tilting his head back to peek beneath the blindfold he put the tail right on the donkey where it belonged. Everyone but me applauded. Indeed, none of them seemed to mind. To me it seemed unbearably unjust. But they just seemed to expect it.

By the time we were told that Ashley, being the birthday boy, would be the first to swing at the piñata, I was unable to control myself any longer.

SIX O'CLOCK COULD HARDLY COME SWIFTLY ENOUGH AFTER THE PIÑATA. Six o'clock, when Alcie finally arrived to take me home. Pinky had wangled a ride from us, and she was waiting in the living room where several other mothers who had arrived earlier were sitting comfortably, sipping some dark liquid from small round glasses. As Edna the maid led me in from the kitchen—where she'd smiled and sneaked me some ice cream and cake even though I'd been isolated from the other children after the piñata incident—Pinky gave me a shy smile, warm but hidden from the panel of mothers.

"Thank you so much for being willing to take Pinky home," Mrs. Packard said to Alcie.

"I'm happy to help." She paused. She sensed something in the postures of the seated mothers. "So. Was the party successful?"

"Oh, yes. Very. No problems at all. Nothing more than could have been predicted." Mrs. Packard, too, paused. "Am I correct in understanding that you are in birth control?"

"I'm the head of Porfea, yes. At Syntex."

"Por what?"

"Sorry. Population Reduction for East Africa," Alcie replied. "I get so used to people *knowing* . . ."

"Necessary work," Mrs. Packard said.

"Yes," Alcie replied. "I like to think it helps."

I tugged at Alcie's skirt. I wanted to get out of there. I felt as though I were being toasted by the gaze of the other mothers.

"One moment, Endymion," Alcie said, shaking me loose from her skirt. "He must have had a good time," she said. "Obviously, he can't wait to tell me about it. You did have a good time, didn't you?" she said, looking at me.

I nodded, yes, hoping Mrs. Packard would not contradict me, counting on the fact that she was too formal and polite to do that.

"I am sure he did," Mrs. Packard said.

"Well, thank you for inviting us to Ashley's party. It was very kind of you. I can tell he enjoyed it. Didn't you?"

Still speechless, I nodded again, though a little less emphatically than she expected. I felt increasingly shy under the scrutiny of all these women, who seemed so comfortable that they might have been in their own homes.

"What do we say?"

"Thank you, Mrs. Packard," I said.

"Pinky? Ah. Why don't you and Endymion wait for us outside?" Mrs. Packard said.

Taking my mother's elbow, she edged her toward the front door behind us. "Endymion is such an unusual name," she said to Alcie. "But then, he's rather an unusual child, isn't he? He has so much . . . energy."

I couldn't hear what was said next, but when Alcie emerged she was saying that they didn't really talk about it much with me and Mrs. Packard gave her a bright look as though some suspicion she had was confirmed by this admission.

"Yes. Of course. Well, good-bye, dear. And good luck," she added.

I dreaded telling Alcie the truth about Ashley's party, so I was grateful that Pinky led Alcie on a merry chase down through the hills to the flatlands. We circled around unnecessarily, Pinky chattering the entire time about the party. It was obvious that Alcie was taken with Pinky. She didn't mind the misdirections and false turns.

"What a nice little girl," she said after Pinky had thanked her twice for the ride and closed the door. Her crinoline petticoat bounced as she skipped up the walk to her front door. Alcie waited until Pinky opened the door, turned and waved prettily, and then closed the door before she drove away.

"She's so polite and sweet," Alcie said. "And I think she's rather pretty, too, don't you?"

"She likes art," I said.

I went over the events of the party in my mind. It was all a jumble. Looking at it from Alcie's point of view, I thought maybe that knocking Edsel's croquet ball into the stream and then pushing him in after it as he tried like a weenie to fish it out wasn't a wrong thing to do. But jeez, Edsel was such a priss, walking around with his mouth pursed in an oval as though he were chanting the mantra of his people. And then only Pinky—thank heavens for her!—seemed to appreciate my laughing at where I'd put the donkey's tail, announcing, "Oops! I gave it a donk!" Leland, who was the kind of kid who is so nice but so needy and weak that you want to pounce on him and thrash him politely about the nose, had shuddered over the word "donk" somewhat overdramatically, I thought. And I just knew that Alcie would never understand how happy I was to be there. How much I liked it there. How I thought it was wonderful to live amongst such luxury, with men and women and gardeners to see that things got done—how easy it would be for me to be rich like that. And she definitely would not understand how much I hated myself for feeling that, how somewhere deep down inside my heart it felt like a betrayal of who I was and of who Albert was and that in order to battle back against the comfort, drunk with luxury and not a little envy, I had grabbed the piñata stick and, whooping and hollering, chased them all off the veranda into the tennis court where I held them hostage until the gardener had whispered behind me, *"No quieres hacerlo, hijo. Dejalo. ¿Entiendes?"*

Alcie could tell from my silence that something had not been quite right and she persisted in prying, asking me the same questions from every possible angle that she could imagine. It made me sad to realize, for the very first time, that my own mother was not able to imagine the right point of view. So with the sadness I had felt the first time I realized that Albert and Alcie would die one day, that they were mortal and imperfect, I just kept repeating that we played games and Ashley won them all and then we all were fed ice cream and cake and then I waited with Edna, their maid, for her to come pick me up.

I could tell she was disappointed. I realized that my going to Ashley Packard's birthday party was almost as important to her as she, herself, going to it, and if I told her the truth, I would take that pleasure away from her. I didn't want to do that. It seemed as though Alcie had little enough pleasure in her life—and never any real joy, if joy requires the expression of it for it to exist.

On the other hand, how many stories had Albert told me in which speaking the truth was important. Whether people liked to hear it or not. Courage, Albert had said, is a matter of heart, and heart demands the truth if it's going to remain healthy. So, when Alcie had settled in front of the television set and was on her second glass of wine, I went in and sat down, tense, expectant, waiting for a commercial to begin. "Mom," I said, finally. And then slowly, carefully, sad over what I was taking away from her and wincing because what I was taking away hurt me, too, I began to tell her what really happened at the party. She looked annoyed, then surprised, then hurt. Finally, she just looked worried.

"I don't understand it," she said. "Where did I go wrong? You're such a good boy. Or you were. What happened to make you misbehave like that?"

I shrugged.

"After all the work I've done," she said. "You do this to me. What was the matter? Didn't you like the other children?"

If you really want to know, I thought, as images of the Lone Ranger and Tonto together out on the prairie played through my imagination— "I guess I felt. . . ."

"Just what could you have felt, Endymion," Alcie said angrily. "Tell me."

I remembered what Ashley had called me to his mother. "I felt like Tonto in town," I said.

"Indians again," Alcie muttered. "Goddamn your father. Listen, Endymion. It's true you're part Indian. Half. But only half. You're also French, Scottish, and a whole lot of other things."

I gave her a weak grin. I may not have known what I was. But I knew what I wanted to be.

"Only half," she repeated. Recovering her self-control, she added, smiling, "We just have to hope you got the good half and not the bad, huh?"

THE NEXT MORNING WAS SUNDAY. IT DIDN'T SURPRISE ME AT ALL THAT Alcie pretended to be bright and chipper, feeding me cereal and then sending me outside to play. That was her way of dealing with the fact that suddenly there was something between us that she wanted to ignore. She hoped it would just go away. And I have to say that I wished it would, too. To her, I guess, my behavior at the Packard house was a blow against the careful way she had tried to raise me, an impossible probability that she had guarded against as carefully as she could. She and I would never speak about it directly again.

It was Albert who surprised me. Alcie must have told him something, that despite all her care I was starting to exhibit tendencies which were aggressive and mean and primitive. I suspected she had sent him out to talk to me. To straighten me out.

He stood there, watching me for several minutes. I ignored him as long as I could. I galloped about the backyard shooting fake arrows from imagined bows and firing bullets from pretend rifles, playing Cowboys and Indians with a vengeance, hoping and wishing that if the Indians kept losing to the cowboys, reality would eventually take firm hold on my imagination, and Alcie would be vindicated.

"What are you playing?" he asked quietly.

I galloped over to him, pulled back on the reins, and skidded my horse to a stop in front of him. "Cowboys and Indians," I said.

"Which are you?"

"Both," I said, annoyed at him for calling me over just as the Indians were trying to escape the corral the cowboys had locked them into.

"Oh?"

"Yeah," I said angrily. "I play the Indians first and then the cowboys."

"Who wins?"

"The cowboys."

"Always?" he asked. There was something in his voice that made him seem genuinely interested.

"Always," I said. Then I relented. My anger lifted. "Well, almost always."

"Ah. Almost always," he said. "So sometimes the Indians win?"

"Yeah," I said. I was prepared for what he was going to say next.

But he only stood there, momentarily satisfied, his hands in his pockets. "Good," he said. And he turned and went back to the house.

So Much Water, Underground

Rhonda and Jim had accepted and canceled, accepted and canceled, and several months had passed since Harry and I had sat around and told stories and blown some weed with them. "A little P.P.," as Harry liked to called it. "A little pee-pee, anyone?" he'd ask. He'd seen *Dances with Wolves* and loved it, and now his bong was not a bong but a peace pipe. I dreaded his saying something like that to Rhonda. She was Osage, I think—all I know for sure is that she wasn't Sioux like in the movie, which she'd told me over the phone when I'd told her we'd gone to see it. I don't think she liked the Sioux very much, although she was nice enough to say that the Sioux weren't the Sioux, not as they were in the movie—which she called "Dunces with Wolves." I could tell by the way she said it that she didn't like the movie much. Something in it must've insulted her, but I didn't ask, and I could only hope that Harry wouldn't bring it up. He loved *Dances with Wolves* even more than *Terminator 2*. And you know how Harry can get going if you disagree with him about a movie and make just about everyone but me hate him.

Me, too, sometimes.

Anyway, Rhonda and Jim were there. Like every couple, they'd had their troubles, but everything seemed to be all right now. Rhonda had seemed almost shy, when they arrived, like she was pregnant or something and didn't want her best friend to know. James had taken up the slack. He's tall and thin and some women think he's good-looking and he knows it enough that he gets along anywhere as long as there are a couple of women around. He'd kept us rolling on the floor with his stories. He'd just finished telling one about some woman in his office who called their boss's wife to thank her for dinner the night before and ask if it was possible to get the recipe for that delicious fruit salad.

"You imagine?" James asked, out of breath. "She thought there was a recipe. For fruit salad."

We fell quiet, after all our laughter.

"Would anyone like a. . . ." —I held my breath as Harry grinned at me; he knew I was worried—. "Refill?" he asked. He went to the kitchen for ice.

"No, thanks," Rhonda said.

"We'd maybe better go," James said, adjusting the pillow he sat on and glancing over at Rhonda.

"Not yet," I pleaded. "Please?"

I waited. Rhonda shrugged as if she didn't care either way. As if going and staying were one and the same to her. I really wanted her to stay. When they went, Harry and I were due to have more words, to finish the fight we'd been into before they arrived.

"Hey. Rhonda's not told one yet," Harry called from the kitchen. He was a little miffed at her quietness. It always miffed him. People came over and smoked his stuff, drank his booze, and ate his food. Listened to him make a fool of himself telling stories, and never said a word.

Rhonda didn't look sour, but lost. Like she felt all alone and resented feeling that way. She cocked her head at Harry's voice, as though she could hear only the gaggles of geese fleeing southward, outside. His Master's Voice, like that Dalmatian in the RCA ad, tipping his ear to the horn on the Victrola. That's the way she looked. She had a way of looking like that and it impressed me always as what people must mean by a different drummer.

Rhonda tried to laugh. "I'm too loaded," she said. "I can't."

"Come on, Rhonda," Harry said, coming back in and plopping down. "Don't be a. . . ." He dropped the ice bucket hard on the glass-topped table.

"Careful, clumsy," I said quickly. "You'll break the table."

Oooh, did he give me a look. I gave him a stonewall back.

Harry dropped new cubes into Rhonda's glass, then Jim's. "Ooops," he laughed. "Guess I'm a little high myself." He laughed again, picked up the cube that had missed Jim's glass, and tossed it at the empty chip bowl. It missed, slid across the glass, and fell into Rhonda's lap. She picked it off her woven skirt without thinking and added it to her glass.

"Some more of this?" Harry asked. He held up the whiskey bottle.

Jim looked quickly at Rhonda and then nodded. He held out his glass. "Where'd you get this brand?" he asked. "It's pretty good. But I've never heard of it before."

It was some brand like James Pepper. Harry has a dream of owning every kind of whiskey ever made. The label on this one was picked away around the edges like it'd been nibbled by mice. It wasn't Chester's Grave. Chester Graves had given me the runs once, so I know it wasn't that.

"Harbormaster brought it aboard one time," Harry said. "Forgot all about it 'till we were cleaning up the boat and I decided to bring all the liquor home." Then he turned to me.

"Remember Josh?"

That was our harbormaster. How could I forget Josh? But Harry didn't know about that.

"Well, Rhonda? Come on," Jim said.

"She used to be the life of parties," Harry said. "What's the matter, James? You been keeping her up too late?"

Jim shifted on his cushion, stuck his finger into his drink, and shoved the cubes around. He sat forward, his back straightened, stiff like a kid about to hear a lecture from his parents about how hard they had it during the Great Depression.

Harry looked around, grinning that grin he gets. "What happened to the old Rhonda? The fun girl we used to know and love?"

"Harry," I said, poking him. "Maybe she wants to be left alone."

"Will you cut that out?" he said to me, his grin a sneer. "She's thinking about something. Aren't you, Rhonda?"

"Okay," Rhonda said suddenly. She sounded determined, like someone who's been trying to avoid a fight and finally puts up her fists. "Okay."

She held out her tumbler at arm's length to Harry, who popped the cork and poured out three or four fingers. Enough to keep her going.

"Remember when we all lived in South San Francisco?"

"Remember," Harry said. "Who could forget those times. We were all just starting out, all four of us. Head over heels for each other then, weren't we? Such kids." He lifted the Naugahyde footstool with his foot, pulled it close to him to lean on, then settled in to hear Rhonda's story, the look on his face waiting to figure out whether it was going to be funny or serious.

"Those shithole apartments we had," Jim said. "Was I ever glad to get out of those. Cops at 2 A.M., waking us up every time some clown pulled the trigger on another one of that woman's lovers. Jeez."

As though she hadn't been interrupted, Rhonda went on, "Remember the water temple we all used to go to?"

"The Hetch-Hetchy," I said.

"Hetch-Hetchy," Harry laughed. "Ever wonder where they got a stupid name like that?"

"It's an Indian name," Rhonda said quietly.

"Well, it's still stupid," Harry muttered sheepishly.

Rhonda looked over at me and then looked real far away like someone who's been locked in a dark closet for a long time and suddenly the door opens and she stands there in the light. It was a funny look, like she was talking to somebody we couldn't see.

"Just after I married James, I went up to the water temple with an old boyfriend. I'd promised. Before I'd gotten married, I'd promised him one last afternoon. He was Osage, too. We were friends and he just wanted to be sure I was happy.

"You remember how the water hits that cement wall inside the temple as it rushes out of the underground aqueduct? How it boils over into the well of the temple and then runs out glassy on the other side, down to the reservoir?"

Rhonda leaned forward and shook a cigarette from Harry's pack and tried to light it. Her hand was shaking and she had trouble hitting the cigarette with the flame.

"There was this man. He was staring down into the well of the temple when I came up to look."

"I've gotta take a whiz," Harry interrupted. He got up. "Wait until I get back?"

"Power," Rhonda said. Harry plopped back down and crossed his legs, afraid he'd miss something if he went to the bathroom. "I'm looking at all that power, hypnotized, and this man says to me like he's reading my mind, 'Fascinating, isn't it? Almost makes you want to jump in.'

"He seems nice enough, but I don't say anything yet because he's a stranger, after all. I look around to see where Charlie is. He isn't too far away, down by the long reflecting pool below the temple. From the frozen way he stands gazing into the pool he seems as fascinated by its stillness as I feel with that white water. I decide that with Charlie so close, it's okay.

"I can hardly hear the man over the roar of the water. His mouth opens wide and he speaks slowly and I realize that he must be shouting as loudly as he can. Still, he manages to make his voice sound gentle. He seems, in fact, real nice.

"'You know it comes all the way from the Sierras underground?' he says. He points down into the deep well of the temple. 'The water. Runs underground clear from the Sierra Madres. All the way across California. Comes out here. Amazing, isn't it? The river runs contained, trapped inside a tunnel, unaware of itself. Of its power. Runs all this way and then bursts out here. That's why the temple, you see.'

"I didn't see. I still haven't said anything to him. But I look back down into the temple. The water looks so furious. Like it is boiling up from the hot core of the world. The man is right. A part of me wants to throw myself down there. Into the whiteness and foam. I want to be taken and tumbled by it out into the glassy stream flowing softly down to the reservoir. I want to find out what it's like in the center of all that foam and force. That passion and release. I try to lean over and put my head down in and hear nothing but the roar of the water, but I'm scared.

"'I used to wonder if the temple was a shrine to the containment or the outbreaking,' he says. Then he thinks a moment. He asks, 'Listen. Do you want to be alone? I don't mean to bother you. To interfere. I'll go, if you like. Just be careful. Okay?'

"'No,' I yell. 'No, don't leave me. I want someone to hold me. I want to lean over and listen but I need someone to hold me. Will you?'

"He seems a bit nervous about that. But he does it. He puts his hands here, on my waist. Just the fingertips, at first. Then the palms. His hands are big. Not fat or puffy, but long. Big. They feel strong like he's been a sailor or a blacksmith. I kept leaning farther and farther down toward the water, him behind me, holding me, until my legs actually leave the ground. I'm not afraid, either, because I can feel those hands holding on to my waist, the way they are holding me."

Harry says, "I was wondering when this story was going to get going." I glare at him and he doesn't laugh. Harry is always laughing, but he doesn't now. "Well?" he says.

"Well, he begins to pull me up again. I don't want him to, you see. It's something I've never felt. The noise is so great but so peaceful, too. It's like the temple is my head and I've forgotten everything except the sound. Forgotten getting married, forgotten work, forgotten Charlie and all the other men I've ever known. Everything except the sound and his hands is washed out of my head and I like that. It feels so good. I want to stay there.

"He begins pulling me back, gently. Slowly and gently. I start kicking and screaming, even though I would drown if he let go. He pulls me out and I start pounding on his chest with my fists and screaming at him to let me go. He stands there and lets me. He even seems to smile slightly as if he'd expected this outburst. 'No,' he says over the noise of the water, 'no,' and I stop hitting and cry and sob and hold on to his neck like I was never going to let go."

Rhonda took a large swallow from her drink. Held it in and swished it around, letting the whiskey seek the dry hidden corners of her mouth, and then gulped it down. The ice rattled as she slid her glass onto the table.

"I didn't want to let go," she said. "Poor man. He was so embarrassed."

She plunged back against the deep cushions of the sofa.

"So what happened?" Harry asked her. "What's the point?"

"I said I was sorry. We sat down on the steps leading up from the reflecting pool to the temple. One thing he said. He said he used to hold his wife like that when he was a younger man."

"You mean he was old?" Harry said.

I said, "It doesn't matter, Harold." I call him by his full name when he's being stupid.

Rhonda went on. "I told him I'd recently married and he said he hoped it would be good for me. I said I was sure it would be. He said that was just the right way to feel. That was the way he had felt before he'd gotten married and it was a good feeling to have. Though marriage could seem like the Hetch-Hetchy at times—running all the way from the mountains and bursting free at the end—it was still the right feeling to have. Though sometimes it did seem to him that it should've been the other way round with the temple at the beginning and not toward the end."

Harry brought out more chips and French dip, and poured more whiskey into everybody's glass. Rhonda's husband was quiet. He shifted his pillow again and began picking at his nails, not looking at anybody. I knew he didn't understand. Neither did Harold. I think I was the only one who understood any of it.

"Go on, Rhonda," I said. "Then what?"

"Not much. Charlie came up the steps and sat with us. The man said it was nice to be young, though he didn't say why at first. I think he thought Charlie was my new husband. I didn't bother, you know, to tell him. It didn't matter. Then he said it was nice to be young, again. You don't know how things can change. How maybe already they have changed.

"He asked us if we'd like to see some snapshots of his wedding. He had some in his car. He carried some with him, these days.

"'Why not?' Charlie said, and the man got up and said he'd be right back.

"We waited. Charlie told me about a little inlet he'd discovered down by the reservoir. I told him about what had happened to me and how the man had held me and didn't he think it was strange. Sweet old Charlie said he didn't know. He said he didn't think it was so strange, but then he hadn't been there."

Rhonda stopped suddenly. She looked down into the palms of her hands.

"So then what happened?" Harry demanded. "Something's got to happen in a story."

"Nothing," Rhonda replied. "He never came back. Nothing happened." She asked me, "You have any memories like that?"

"What? Oh. No," I said quickly. "No, I never."

Harry laughed. "That's a rotten story, Rhonda. I've gotta say that. You used to tell better stories than that."

Rhonda's eyes were squinted and wet, as if she couldn't see anything as close to her as Harold.

"You understand it, Jim?" Harry said.

"I've heard it before." That's all Jim says. My heart near broke the way he says it. It's like hearing a silent spring.

"And you let her tell it again?"

"Harold," I said. "Ssssh."

"Even you tell better stories than that," he said to me. "I'll tell you a real story. Have you heard this one, Jim?"

Jim gulped the last of his drink.

"Here," Harry said, holding out the bottle to him, "have another and listen to this."

"No, thanks," Jim says. "Another time maybe. We better be going. Let's go, okay, Rhonda?"

Harry stood there after helping Rhonda on with her coat and shutting the door. When he turned, he said, "Well, where were we? I've got a few things to add. Like your interrupting me all the time, like your calling me 'Harold,' as if I don't know."

"Not now, Harry. Please? Just go to bed."

I collected the plates and dip bowls, the crumbs of chips scattered around the table, and plucked the larger crumbs from the carpet. I'd vacuum tomorrow. I took all the dishes in, though, and began to wash. When I was done, I took them all out of the drainer, put them on the right side of the sink, and washed everything again. It felt like I couldn't get them clean enough.

Afterward, I slouched in the living room, thinking. I had lied when I told Rhonda no. I lit up my first cigarette in a year. It made me cough but I was determined to finish it. Fuck it, I thought. Just fuck it.

Harry came in wearing his bathrobe, his hairy legs below the hem. He was still pretty worked up. Still wanting to fight.

"You coming to bed? Or you gonna sleep out here?"

"I'll be in," I assured him softly. I didn't feel like fighting.

The first time I was held, Ralph had put his hands on my hips just the way Rhonda had said. I could feel him, running his hands up my back. He put his arms as far around me as he could and held me. Not the way Harry does when he wants to have sex, squeezing my ribs together. Just held.

You're fooling yourself, I thought. It wasn't ever that way. But my bones seemed to remember something. My bones seemed to want something. Why hasn't it ever felt the same? Was it just because it was the first time? Couldn't it happen again? I felt like I was going to burst, thinking about it.

Harry was snoring loudly, the way he does. The bedroom had an eerie cast, lit by the test pattern on the TV. It's a new TV. Harry bought it because we watch so much of it.

I sat on my side of the bed. I stared at Harry's back a long time, and it made me sad. I lifted his arm out from beneath the covers and looked at his hand. His snoring stopped. I thought about Rhonda's story some more, and I thought of Ralph, and I began to cry, the inside of my head hurting, roaring like Rhonda's water temple.

In the middle of the night, I woke up with hot fingers pressing my hips like pokers. They weren't Harry's. They weren't anyone's. That was the problem with it. They weren't anyone real's. I could tell it was going to keep me awake a lot.

Tarantulas

For Jack

I WORK AT THE POST OFFICE, MAIN BRANCH, SACRAMENTO. WORKED, rather, since I was caught last week, and today—but no! I want to tell you about the letters. They're the ones to blame, I think, for my being here. And it looks like I'll be here or somewhere like it a long time.

I hate this city. Sacramento is called—by natives and immigrants alike—the "armpit of the West." I don't know what that makes L.A., but about Sacramento, they're right. It draws dogs, drunks, and demons to it like iron filings, to poke through the rubble of urban renewal, to wander through the park surrounding the capitol by day, or to hover shapeless in alleys and dark corners by night. But I don't hate them anymore. I hate the stupidity of the people, of the system that lets a cretin get a job for better pay than me, and then neither the cretins nor the system will leave you alone. . . .

I sorted mail for the northern San Joaquin Valley—Saint Joke, I called it, because the other is Mexican. All the mail with "95" as the first

two numbers of the zip code comes into Sacramento and then is
resorted for the surrounding towns—Winters, Davis, Folsom, whatever.
I used to deliver mail until someone took a shot at me in the MacArthur
district, where they don't like lighter-skinned people much, not even
mailmen, since all they bring are bills, junk mail, late unemployment
checks, and at rare times a personal letter from the world outside. But
that shot scared me, coming out of nowhere and ricocheting off the dirt
of an empty lot. One shot. It never happened again, but it was enough
to make me happy when my transfer to the mailroom came through. I
no longer had to weave down the sidewalk, alert and changing the
length of my stride like they taught me in the marines, looking into dark
faces which stared at me, blank, but not indifferent. Faces I wanted to
tell, "I understand, I'm on your side," framed by ears that would not
have heard.

At first, I was pretty good at it, sorting. After all, I wanted with all
my life to be there, and I could spot, read, and sort the third and fourth
numbers faster than anyone. I even got to work the second shift, and
had as a result moments of privacy, which I used to think things through,
to make plans, while mechanically doing my job. Why I got bored, I
don't know, but about six months ago I began to take an interest in the
letters and cards I was sorting, starting to imagine the things they contained, the people they were from, and the people they were to.

The first one that caught my eye was only a postcard. It read (I
remember them all), "Dear Walt, got your letter a week ago, and you're
right" (about what, I wondered then, conscious that I was pausing in my
routine). "Your suspicion that my prolonged silence means something,
is right. It's happening all over again—a lot like before—and I can tell
from my loss of humor and my difficulty in writing to my friends,
because I don't understand *why* it's happening. And this time it is the
same twingy feeling, but different, mostly because it's happened before,
as you know all too well, and this time I can see it coming a long way
off. Forgive the terse card. I'll write when I can. My best to Melissa—

tell her the work being done here doesn't compare to hers. Neither do the workers. Best, C." What was it? I wondered. It was like a code, and although I understand it now, the privacy of it made me angry, or was I afraid? Presumably, Walt, and indirectly Melissa, understood what it meant.

I dropped the card on the floor and kicked it out of the way until I had time to pick it up and reread it. I noted the return address before I dropped it in the right bag. That was Friday. I remember because the next night Karen remarked that I seemed distracted, as if I wasn't with her, or even at her party, which was celebrating the summer solstice (in California, anything can be celebrated). At the same time I thought it was because I was at her party, with her friends and not my usual ones, and I hadn't felt like going in the first place, but had said yes because my steady date, Allyn, was out of town. Now that I think about it, though, I know that my mind was still occupied with that card, and so, when Karen said "You were a big help" to me after her friends had gone home, I didn't stay around to fight it out with her, but suggested that she not invite me again. She never did, by the way.

(I find it odd that only Allyn has been to visit me since last week when they came and got me. The rest of my friends—and I had a lot of them, believe me—have let her carry their concern for them. It was she who noticed the tree which is planted outside my window, and it seemed to bother her. You can see the trunk of it, since where I am is sunk halfway into the ground. The feet of people move past the window between me and the tree fairly often, and once in a while a dog stops to sniff at it. I am learning a lot about people from their shoes; they tell you as much as a postcard, anyway.)

THE SECOND CARD FROM C. WAS LARGER. ONE OF THOSE TWENTY-TWO-cent ones. I had begun to worry by then that I would miss the next one; I hadn't realized how much, until it was in my hand. I nearly froze.

I was disappointed. With all the extra space, the card was pretty matter-of-fact, with only one or two allusions to "it's going on." The rest was the weather and thanks for writing (it was to Melissa, as I recall). I almost didn't send it on because, after all my excitement, I felt cheated by C. (when I began to call him "Chris," I don't remember), as if he had promised me something that he hadn't delivered. But it was not the end. No, this card promised a letter within the month, and so I sent it on and was patient and waited.

(The public defender has just been in. He seemed relieved when he asked me how I wanted to plead and I said, "Guilty, of course." He laughed when I added, "How guilty, though, I don't know." He, the public defender, is a misshapen little man—a dwarf or a midget. I never could decide which was which. He wheels about in one of those fancy electric wheelchairs, and thus is afraid of anything but level ground. His body looks like it's been hung for years by a hook through the left shoulder, and so he even sits tilted. I felt sorry for him. And I was happy that I seemed to cheer him up.

Allyn wasn't nearly as much fun. "Why did you do it?" she asked. I said nothing. What could I say? Allyn works for one of the state offices here, and she is very regular and decent. She doesn't even mind going to work on sunny fall days. How could I expect her to understand?

"A mistress, I could have understood," she complained. I'll bet. "But all this time, it was only someone else's letters. Strangers." I started to protest, and then let it go.

"Letters," she said in disgust. I asked her to wear her black skirt with something yellow and red, if she came again. She was confused, but I think she will do it.

If you lie on my cot, you can see the branches, set off by the sky. They seem far away.)

I WAITED AND WAITED FOR THE PROMISED LETTER, WHICH DID NOT COME within the month. Had the card said within *a* month and not *the* month? It made a difference, but one which was initially so small that I hadn't paid close attention—my memory is otherwise excellent. But the anxiety of being caught reading mail, I suppose, had caused me to overlook the importance of one tiny word. It was then that I hit upon my idea to borrow the letters and make copies, before sending them on to Walt and Melissa.

The letter came, and it was as if someone knew I was doing this, because the letter was turned around in the bundle, facing the wrong way, so that the first words I saw were on the back of the envelope. "The stamp, somehow, seems appropriate." I recognized the handwriting immediately, and I could feel my own pulse as I turned over the envelope. The stamp was a recent issue, of General Washington praying on one knee at Valley Forge. Another mystery, perhaps solved inside the letter. I looked around (were they watching me, even then?), conscious that I was staring. Nobody seemed to be paying attention, and before it was too late I tucked the letter into my hip pocket beneath my sweater, and prayed it didn't show.

All day the letter pressed against my hip, making me conscious of it, bulging out the pocket with its bulk as if to accuse me. I tried not to act differently on the way home, and I carried off the usual how-are-you's with the bus driver, but the derelict who sat across from me seemed to know I'd done something wrong, staring at me as if I exuded an odor he recognized, finally asking me could I spare fifty cents for a man down on his luck, and grinning when I gave him a dollar—one of those grins which shows only the incisors. I jumped off the bus two blocks before my stop. I could feel him watching me as I walked into the foyer of an apartment building and waited until the bus was out of sight.

I sneaked up to my room quietly (I live, or lived—I keep forgetting—in one of those boardinghouses run by one of those nice old couples who have been caught in the exhalation of the city as it overgrows their neighborhood, who can no longer afford the taxes on the property they were once happy to own, but can't afford to move away, and who hope they will die before the city comes around to tell them they must retreat in front of progress). Drawing the drapes, I put a kettle on my portable burner while I showered, and then I sat before it, carefully steaming the envelope open, impatient, but forcing myself to do a good job before opening it.

"Dear Walt [it read],

"Why is it that people will not leave you alone? I know what you'll say, so I don't even know if I'm asking a real question. You'll laugh when I tell you that I seem to have been cast into the role of a supreme egoist, because I haven't the time to waste. One woman accused me of not caring for people because she told me she was depressed and I said something like 'We all get depressed, don't we.' Jesus, they think that to burden you with their stupid problems is friendship. Another guy called me a bastard because I had a small showing of my stuff downtown—I think he thought my showing accused him of something? Tarantulas all. . . .

"Did I ever tell you about the time I had a tarantula crawl across my chest, when I was a boy? Cured me of tree-climbing. Some friends of my adoptive parents had a citrus grove out towards the desert, south of L.A. I'd climbed shirtless into the "Y" of a low tree—I can't remember what kind of tree—and was sitting there, arms out, holding on to branches on either side of me, looking at the way the flat sky gave the trees relief. I felt something tickly moving down my right arm, and when I turned to look there was this monstrous hairy brown thing with unending legs, crawling across my arm toward my heart. I did the right thing: I froze. I even stopped breathing. Have you ever considered how slowly a tarantula moves? I dove out of the tree as soon as it was beyond my hand, stumbled off a few steps, and collapsed, crying, without sound, without tears. It makes me nervous, now. But that tarantula made me very silent out of fear and hatred for the ugly thing which had tormented me without knowing it was tormenting me. It's that silence I paint out of, now.

"What's that got to do with anything? Nothing; or maybe everything, since it's the kind of feeling I had when I had to leave Davis, and I'm beginning to have it again. I am trying to control it. We'll see. Keep in touch. Write words when you can. Back to work. Best always, C."

I had just finished copying the letter, having read it over a couple of times, when Allyn called to find out why I was late. I'd forgotten I'd promised to come over after work. "I'm sick," I groaned. I didn't dare tell her the truth.

"Do you want me to come there?"

"I think I'll be okay. And you know it bothers the Pasadas" (my landlords). Fortunately, this was the truth, as Allyn knew. Although the Pasadas made exceptions in certain circumstances.

"You will make the party Saturday night?"

I'd forgotten about that, too. Shit. "As long as I'm well," I said, trying to sound convincing. She didn't trust my voice; neither did I. She said she loved me, and I should go right to bed. I agreed, and returned to my letter. First, though, I pulled the venetian blinds so the light slanted up and not down toward the street (Allyn wasn't the nosy or suspicious type, but you couldn't be sure), and lit the hurricane lamp the Pasadas provided every room for use in case of a black- or brownout (they are Latin Catholics, and definitely dislike the dark), turning the wick as far down as possible, so the ceiling wouldn't smudge.

I recopied the letter, practicing the handwriting and etching the words into my memory, since I had always intended to destroy the copies. Why didn't I? If you need to ask, well . . . let me put it this way, Why should I have?

(I am putting in just as much detail as I think necessary. I have an idea to read this at my trial, not to defend myself, but to explain as much as possible. I want them to understand as much as they can.)

SEVERAL OTHER LETTERS CAME, ALL SHORT, CRYPTIC, UNIMPORTANT.

(Allyn, black skirt with rust-colored piping, yellow blouse: "Is that why you borrowed my car?"

I said nothing. My face must have looked hopeful, though. Was she beginning to understand for herself?

"Let me get it straight. You took these letters, copied them, even corrected them, adding things to them, before mailing them on? Then on weekends, you borrowed my car to go visit some friends?" I smiled. "And what you did was drive out to Davis and watch the house the letters were delivered to?"

I had to get to know them, too, didn't I? It would've been like writing to an empty space, a vacuum, if I hadn't.

"Which letters were the originals. The ones they found in your room, or. . . ."

I said nothing. Did it matter? The ones which arrived were obviously the right ones. Was it so difficult for them to understand that? I asked Allyn to find out what kind of tree that was, outside my window.

"You don't seem to realize!" she yelled.)

LET'S SEE. I'M GETTING CONFUSED. TIME MEANS SO LITTLE IN HERE, AND people keep interrupting. This one comes to mind:

"Dear Walt,

"Well, it's happened. I feel a certain kind of relief over it all—it's happened, it's over, and I don't need to keep constant watch on it. But I want you to know I did try. I really did. Last year, when I arrived here, the first thing I did was tell everyone that I was dull, with the hope that they would not invite me to their parties (they call them that, but the word is questionable—more like interrogations, social trials). Now that I look back, I realize that they could not believe me—not because it wasn't true—but because for them to accept that I was dull meant that they had to change their perspective on themselves, ask themselves if they weren't dull, too. (And we know what perspective can do, right?) Why else would a self-confessed dullard not wish to be invited to their parties?

"So, the Director of Visual and Performing Arts had his party—the invitations are more like a warrant, they don't ask for an RSVP. Jenny went with me (even though I begged her to stay home, which, after last year's party, was what she wanted). We went with our only friend here— a terribly decent fellow, born with a Guggenheim in his mouth (he deserves one; damned good lithographer).

"Anyway, the Director. He's an insidious, hairy man—one of those throwbacks in appearance. After my first year here, I knew he was basically harmless; his real ability to poison has—I'm tempted to say evolved, but that's not accurate—homogenized right out of him. He would remind you, too, of a tarantula, all appendage and no body to speak of.

"I can hear Jenny crying in bed; it's obviously upset her. I ramble, anyway. I'll mail this tomorrow, and write the rest soon. Give my love to Melissa and anyone else you think appropriate. Affectionately, C."

Each time I copied the letter, I felt . . . what? Disturbed, I guess. Not cheated, although the letter seemed less than complete, and I wanted to fill in things. I could not have gone on copying, anyway, because it tired me. I blew out the lamp and tried to sleep, but I couldn't for the things which crawled around my sheets, the almost silent spinning which was going on in the dark corners. I got dressed and went out.

It was the middle of the night, and Sacramento had gone to bed, for the most part. I walked familiar neighborhoods at first, looking for a friend who was still awake; I didn't have a friend whom I could awaken in the middle of the night, and especially not one I could tell what was happening to me. One I could trust. Not Allyn, that was for sure.

The sick, the trod upon, the poor—they seem to stay up later. I began to pass groups of three, four, sitting on steps and porches, watching nothing quietly. Did they know something I didn't, something I hadn't even suspected until then? I liked the darkness: I'd never known this before. But I'd never walked this late before, either. The darkness was something anyone could keep to himself.

A gang of kids passed me, across the street. "Hey," one called out. I thought of running. A solitary man to my left rocked forward like he was nodding with his whole body, and I realized the kid was greeting him. I wasn't alien there; it was like I was invisible. . . .

(MY ATTORNEY HAS JUST LEFT. HE BROUGHT ME A "CARE" PACKAGE— cookies, sausage, cheese, cigarettes, soap. His mother had made it up for me. I don't smoke, but I was grateful anyway. I offered him some sausage, but he waved it away with the prosthesis which is his left arm, grinning. "Do you know a Karen Johnson?" he asked.

"Once."

He grinned and nodded, his legs swinging slightly from the edge of his chair. I was beginning to like him. His odd humor, and his deformity, appealed to me. We got along.

"Why?" I asked.

"She's going to testify."

"She's going to testify," I repeated. "She doesn't need to try to help me."

"No, no. No, no, no, no, no," he said. "For the prosecution." His mouth stretched the syllables of the word out, relishing each one. "Now." He became serious. "Do you want to plead insanity? With what she's gonna say, it would be easy. Allyn, too."

Allyn, too? I thought.

"She's for us. But it doesn't matter. She wants to tell the court that you were definitely not yourself, for the last several months."

I was silent. He watched me for a long time, as I felt the realization begin to crawl up my spine. I'd never been more myself. But they were going to deny that, weren't they? Bury me with details, circumstances. "I can't," I said wearily.

"Well," he said. "Your choice. You can always change your mind, you know." He pointed at the cookies with his prosthesis, and I gave him one. "Tell me something," he munched. "The inspector found a postcard in your room that said C. was fine, had cut out drinking—a lot of things like that. The inspector also found the phony cancel stamp you made. Pretty good job, by the way. Who wrote that card?"

"Chris. C."

"Why didn't you mail it on?"

"I thought I had." That isn't true. I hadn't mailed it because something was wrong with it, my language wasn't right, or else there was something missing—I wasn't sure which—but it gave me that tickly feeling, and I was afraid. I watched my attorney pack up the papers he had in the little case attached to the right side of his electric wheelchair, and whirl to go out.

"Let me know if you'd rather spend some years in Napa instead of Folsom," he said as he left. "Save the state some money. . . .")

IT IS, LITERALLY, THE DEAD OF WINTER OUTSIDE. THE OAK TREE (OR SO Allyn has said, oak) seems close, the only thing that seems close. Everything else seems far away. I was going to ask Allyn to find out his new address from Walt, but I doubted she'd do it. Ah, the last letter, the one they caught me with, I must put that down. I owe it to Chris to do that, at least. Otherwise, they will fill in their own details and bury him with me.

"I am, in some ways, an asshole. I know it. But I cannot control it; I'm not sure I want to control it any longer. Still. . . .

"There I was at the Director's party, yelling at the one person who had been kind to me. Going on about nothing—nothing he could do anything about, anyway—one word leaping up out of my heart after another. He kept saying, Okay, okay, until he found a way to escape through the milling people and not come back. I stood there feeling foolish, as people tried to ignore me. Walt, I was overcome by an utter loneliness such as I have never felt before (except once, as a child), as if I were the central figure in one of those paintings by Munch where all the detail surrounding the figure has been obliterated.

"It was not drunkenness. They could see that; could have excused my outburst, if it had been that. What was it then? Arrogance? I don't think so. Passion? No; well, yes, but of a certain kind they did not know. Fear? Maybe. Maybe. In front of me, a short brunette sat on her heels and laughed and laughed. Behind me, Jenny sat stiffly on the couch, and I think only I could see the tear that slid off the flare of her nose. Both were nervous. I was powerless, could not calm either of them, for each had, in her own way, taken on all the pains that huddled in groups around the room, like small circles trying to overlap each other in the water. I was tired. And I do not believe in pain. . . .

"That was it: tiredness. Tired of being powerless. For what power I had was endowed (and not human), given me by those who held on to it and portioned it out, making me silent with fear and hatred. On the walls, every wall, were Haida prints crowded together, the frames bumping against each other in pretentious disarray, their subtle colors massed together in a common cry for attention. A pale yellow is no longer pale when it joins forces with reds. The delicate black outlines become insidious, dominant where they shouldn't be. It was my eyes that made me drunk, caused me to behave like that. And in my drunken sight it seemed all of us were human shells with the souls of tarantulas, and each time I uttered a word it came out brown and hairy.

"I found Jenny, later, outside in the snow, sitting against a tree in the full moon's yellow light, crying. Not for herself or for me, but for the people still left inside. I stood there, alone and helpless, sheepish and mute, beginning to see that it had begun a long long time ago.

"I am not sorry.

"As I write that, I can feel something has changed, something irrevocable, yet something unknown as yet. Like the threads of one cable suspending a bridge, something has worn through and snapped, and I find myself alone in an odd way. There are only five, maybe six, people I care about in this world (why, Walt, are we scattered all over the globe?). Really care about. The rest are only as real as . . . as the pile of red bricks my neighbor has stacked outside my studio window. Bricks that I know are there, but can't see because it is dark and the light over my desk (one of those lamps which looks like a praying mantis with a glowing head) holds me here, prevents me from seeing past the dim reflection of myself, duplicated in the storm window.

"(A day later). The Director made an appointment with me for tomorrow. You see? They move slowly, but not that slowly. I will go, of course. I know what it is he wants to say, and I know what it means. One last time I must let him run his hairy fingers across my heart. But this time, I am not afraid, though silent and still.

"Funny. My power is to make it easy for him by not breathing.

"Next time I write, it will be from somewhere else. Where? I don't know. Jenny has an idea that we should go to New Mexico and buy an *Abiquiu,* and live and work. At least the tarantulas there are real. How we would live, I don't know, but work is all that matters now (besides Jenny), work and silence.

"Until whenever, she sends her love, as do I. Love, C."

THERE. TONIGHT I WILL CORRECT THIS COPY, AND PRACTICE IT FOR tomorrow. Tomorrow, I must go before them, let them look at me, ask me questions I cannot answer, decide my guilt. I wonder if they will understand that these were not someone else's letters. Perhaps not. Perhaps the judge will want to ask why I did it, and I can read what I have written.

I have begun to like it here. The routine is like any other, but I don't have to see anyone, except my attorney, and even he can be kept out.

The oak stands against the winter, budless. It stands there like a dancer, arms arcing up, the fingers nearly touching high above the trunk. Its roots go far beneath the ground as if the earth has risen like dough around it and me, half sunk in the ground myself, and I can see the beginnings of a crack in the wall where the roots have tried to enter my cell. Yet, if I move on my cot, the image of the tree against the white moon shifts, and if I rock my head, I can make the still dancer dance.

As I look out the window and wonder how guilty I am, and of what, really, I can see against the faraway sky the dark lines which tell me that what they call my crime is delicate and dark and can only be judged—truly judged in detail—against a yellow New Mexico moon.

Early Age and Late Disorder

ORDER CLUNG TO MERRILL LIKE WET FLANNEL. BORN AMONG THE Onandagas, he had always feared disorder, and he had always tried to keep the flannel moist by controlling the dry winds that intruded upon his life. He had always been this way: never had he been late, even though the date on whom he attended like a royal palm might have been; he had had consistent and good grades in college (except in English in which the ambiguities caused a rash to break out around his neck); he had kept himself fit even into the meal-sack years of his forties; and when he had married, he had wedded a white woman who wished above all to keep the top of the stove clean.

He believed he was happy this way. He held to a dream of a Normandy cottage on the coast of Maine. He had a good job with an accounting firm. And he had a comfortable home that was cool in summer and insulated against the central New York winters, inhabited by three of the most charming children any man could want. At the end of each year, he and his wife had enough left to travel to New York City to eat oysters in Grand Central Station. Merrill was, then, what we would call an eminently safe man, although lately he had begun to feel the breath of a cruel force panting just beneath the pleasantness of his world, and he dated the feeling from the first time he had seen the mad-woman on the corner.

He lived in a city of hills and swamps reclaimed from Erie Canal days, and each morning Merrill left home in his new Buick, leaving his wife off at the university, circling back and picking up Joan, his secretary, and descending into another day of figures and—you'd believe it if you made the same journey—peace. By practice and revision, Merrill got the trip down so pat that he would pass through the same intersection only twice.

It was there that the woman had first appeared, her tongue licking out of her mouth at him. He had felt sorry for her at first, and ignored her. But time after time she was there, and lately he began to feel sorrier for himself. Lately, her tongue seemed only for him. He found himself dreading her.

It was March. There was an old man hunched into a flock of woolen coats against the early spring cold, selling colored balloons on the corner. Merrill was anxious that day about his habits, which were changing determinedly, which had been displaced enough lately to notice them. The light was red. Joan got out of the car and bought a blue balloon, speckled with star-like spots of silver. As he watched the old man dipping into the well of his pocket for change, the woman appeared, stepping off the curb in front of his car and sticking her tongue all the way out of her mouth at him, so far that the tongue curved with strain. He felt he had the right to travel unmolested, and the muscles of his leg began to contract, slipping his right foot slowly from the brake pedal, stopping and relaxing again when the woman mouthed something that looked exactly like "son of a bitch."

Why me? Merrill said.

His mother had been like that, he remembered, never making complete sense and doing things in public that disturbed or annoyed him. His mother had finally gone mad; he had spent his entire life training himself to be sane. Merrill's pity and anger passed, and he felt a laugh break loose somewhere in the pit of his stomach and burst upward, dry and parched like a belch. He looked up and away at the stoplight and tapped his fingers on the wheel as though he was listening to the radio. Out of the corner of his eye, Merrill could see the woman back on the curb now. Her face, rounded by baggy fat and poverty, contorted around her tongue, which had reemerged as Joan slid into the car.

My God, Merrill said to himself. Mother. My mother. And she could have been, even though in the heat of his memory, Merrill could not say exactly why.

Passing the second streetlight pole from the corner, he flipped on the turn indicator and glanced at the quartz clock set into the dash. They were a few seconds off schedule and he'd have to pick up speed once around the corner in order to make the green light at the bottom of the hill. He and Frank Todd at the office had a sort of competition about driving through Syracuse with the least number of stops. They had to trust each other, sure, but from time to time one of them checked the other out by driving an acclaimed route. Frank (Joan worked for him, too) had started the whole thing and Merrill knew that when Frank got back after convalescing from his recent accident he'd have a few routes for him to beat. He caught himself starting to stick his tongue out at Frank.

Joan glanced at him as she tied the balloon to the handbrake of the car. Something wrong with your mouth? she asked.

Merrill wondered, as he had wondered before as he'd passed the mental hospital, if they knew one of their people was out. He tried to let the woman slip quietly from his mind, like an irrelevant figure, as he swung up the ramp to the parking garage. Morning, Sid, he said.

Good morning, Mr. Withlesse, Sid said. Miss Spethe. Nice day, huh?

Merrill noticed Sid's slight lisp as if for the first time. He looked up at him in the kiosk with surprised interrogation. Sid was grinning. Nithe day for balloons, he said, and, before Merrill could explain that the balloon was Joan's, he had slipped back into his kiosk with a chortle that sounded like Harth, harth. The arm of the gate went up.

The elevator was packed with people staring at the floor numbers and shifting their weight from foot to foot or coughing when the numbers went dark between floors. Merrill wanted to scream or stick out his tongue or fart. Joan slipped her hand into the ell of his arm.

Merrill, she hissed, it's okay, Merrill. Sid was only trying to be funny.

The doors clambered open and she dragged him into the hall. God, Merrill, she said as the doors sighed shut. What's the matter with you? You realize you were staring at everyone in the elevator and muttering? Make an ass out of yourself. But not me. Okay, Merrill?

Everybody stares at the numbers, Merrill said weakly, half-heartedly trying to defend himself. Had he been muttering?

What are they supposed to do, Merrill? They don't know you and you don't know them. We're all just trying to concentrate on what we've gotta get done before Friday's over, right, Merrill? Bet you wouldn't like it much if some idiot got on poking his tongue out and muttering at you. You're acting pretty funny lately, Merrill.

Merrill shrugged, nodded. He felt like a child in the face of this reprimand. Like some over-large pet. The same way he sometimes thought he got treated at home. Like an old dog no one wanted to care for and that only got in the way. Joan was right. He'd have to watch himself.

Still, going down for lunch, he had to bite his tongue and concentrate on the elevator doors, staring at the seam and waiting for it to yawn and release him from the cage of people. He wanted to tip his hat to them as they got off, but he managed to slug his hands into his jacket pockets and hunch against the blast of cold that came in at them on the lobby floor. He felt as if he had to make a decision, but what or how kept escaping him. It didn't make any sense.

JOAN WAS ALREADY IN FEDELMAN'S OFFICE, SUNK INTO A TAN NAUGA-hyde chair. She gave him a sheepish look as he came in. Fedelman Junior stood at the window, hands clasped behind him with his back to Merrill, surveying greater Syracuse. It was a pose he'd gotten from a movie or television, standing like that in front of his window. Across the street was a shoe factory, a big prison-like building without bars. Beyond it, Merrill could see the huge sign of yellow-orange light bulbs spelling out *Rescue Mission.* In front of the factory was a parking lot, owned, like the office building, by Fedelman Senior.

Merrill waited until Fedelman turned and waved the palm of his hand at a chair. Sit, Merrill. Have a seat, he said.

Merrill remained standing, rubbing his neck. Fedelman leaned stiff-armed on his desk and looked at Merrill slowly, searchingly, and then eased down into his desk chair. A suppressed sigh seemed to come from the chair's padding. Clasping his hands as though he were about to pray, he said, Now, Merrill, let me finish before you feel you have to say anything, but I've been going over the tax figures on the Stavros account. I must say that it doesn't look like your usual job. No, it doesn't. No, no (he said these no's to himself as he leafed through a folder on his desk).

Merrill felt sick, dizzy. He'd better start bringing his lunch, he thought.

Now, Fedelman said. Joan here tells me you've been under some kind of strain. That you and your wife. . . . He held his hand up like a school crossing guard. I don't care what kind of strain and I understand. It happens to all of us. At least it can. But, Fedelman said, but. . . .

A school crossing guard, Merrill thought. Suddenly he longed for the grammar days of sixth grade. A lieutenant in the crossing brigade, he had left the classroom early, slowly donning with self-importance the bright fluorescent safety vest and then the bandolier with its stripes and badge, which distinguished the officers from the privates, the mere handlers of stop signs. They would deploy themselves at the four corners of the school, ready to stop traffic when the school disgorged its children.

He had stood at parade rest, confident in his authority, the whistle he held in his lips animating the younger privates who held stop signs on long poles. On alternate Thursdays, he had stayed late for lectures and lessons on safety given by members of the local police force. In full uniform, the police had worn one large badge on their chests, bright and shining as if divinely forged, and Merrill had dreamed of the day when he, too, would be recognized as one of them.

Sit, Merrill, sit, Fedelman said.

Resenting the tone of this intrusion on his private dream of the past, Merrill stubbornly refused to sit. He had never imagined as a boy that he would come to this. Fedelman droned. Merrill noted that the sign on top of the Rescue Mission had one burnt-out bulb.

Why don't you take a week or two off, Fedelman said. Get things straightened out at home.

JOAN WALKED SOFTLY BESIDE HIM DOWN THE CHUTE OF THE CORRIDOR that led to their offices. You should have sat, she said.

Merrill didn't reply. He glanced at her. He had always thought of her weak chin as cute. Now he realized that what he had seen as cute was really strong, hidden by a double fold of flesh. How long had she been attending night school in accounting? It didn't matter. She was certified. He felt proud of her. She would clean up the mess he'd made of the Stavros account.

You know what those write-offs were for, don't you? Merrill said. Joan didn't want to know.

Business entertainment, she said. Merrill began to suspect that beneath the calm of her voice was a private exultation.

He sat in his office and thought about taking two weeks off from work. He would spend them at home. In the afternoons, he'd drive over and pick up his children from school. Maybe he and Doreen could take a little trip, kind of a second honeymoon. He took a pencil and slid it into the little hole of the gold-plated sharpener Doreen had given him on their fifth anniversary and listened to the motor whir, grinding the pencil down slowly until it was only a tip on the end of the eraser. The motor sounded tired as it shut off.

He got up and paced the width of his office, once stopping by the open door to survey the maze of partitioned cubicles that formed a series of holding pens through which each of the bent heads was driven by some force larger than itself, some getting axed but most of them getting promoted. Joan would be promoted. He didn't mind. He didn't even blame her for being prepared to take his job, if that was what happened. It was what people did. It was the order of things.

Picking a folder from the file cabinet, he dumped its contents on his desk. Then he swept them together in a heap and jammed them back into the folder, which he replaced in its slot. Looking out the door again, he wondered what would happen if the partitions were torn down, and the thought of the disorder that would result astounded him.

For an instant, he was blinded by it. It seemed as if all the employees had raised their heads and were giving him the same ridiculing look. Don't be silly, their looks said, everything would simply grind to a halt.

He staggered back to his desk, trying to assess the power of disorder. From a picture on the desk a pretty brunette and three small children stared at him passively. The frame was chopped-up money sealed in plastic. He had introduced it himself as a promotion. Stavros had one just like it. His wife, had she ever looked like that? And those three tiny figures surrounding her like dwarfed guards defending her from something behind the camera—what had they to do with him sitting behind this desk on top of which they stared? Merrill felt his lungs constrict as though he were being strangled by a large snake as he realized that he couldn't remember the exact ages of his children. He knew they were two years apart the way he and Doreen had planned, and the eldest must be about seventeen. But he wasn't sure without subtracting the year of

his eldest's birth from the current date, and even then the months confused him.

He pressed a button on his phone and watched Miss—or, rather,
Ms.—Thomas stand and turn, and walk toward him past Joan's cubicle.
Ms. Thomas reached in and knocked lightly on his door.

You called, she said flatly. Do you need something?

No, he said. I pressed the wrong button. Then he changed his mind.
Wait, he said. Yes. Close the door, he said, and sit down. He nodded at
the couch across from his desk and turned the photograph down on his
desk so the faces wouldn't see what he was about to do. Please, he said,
and Ms. Thomas's face relaxed.

He smiled. She was attractive because of her assurance, her seeming indifference to promotion and the orderly politics of the office. She
seemed to know that if she played it safe and waited she would be
advanced surely, though perhaps not swiftly. He opened a file folder and
spread it before him, patting it with his hands. Let's see, he said. You've
been with us two years, now, is that correct? Ms. Thomas nodded. You
like it here? Her nod was more hesitant, suspicious. Do you agree that
it's time you were moved up a bit, got a slight raise? Her face twitched.
She ducked her head, spreading the eyelids with her fingers, popped a
contact from her eye and placed it in her mouth, and then reversed the
process and put it back in her eye, carefully.

Well, Merrill said. I like your attitude, and now I'm going to help
you get ahead. Okay?

Ms. Thomas ran the tip of her tongue along the inside of the seam
of her pursed lips.

Merrill told her that he was taking a few weeks off to take care of
some private business. Spontaneously, he devised and explained an intri-
cate filing system that would make parts of every major account he had
handled for two years impossible to find for anyone except Ms. Thomas.
At the end of what proved to be nearly an hour, Ms. Thomas sat looking resigned but expectant, too, as though there had to be more. It might

have been gratitude, but Merrill thought that the relief in her face was for another reason as he told her that would be all and shook her hand and wished her luck.

She paused at the door. Are you sure there's nothing else? she said.

She looked almost disappointed when Merrill said, No, just remember the system. And close the door as you leave, please. He sneered at the bleating of phones and the clatter of typewriters that increased in volume and then died out as she opened and closed the door. He stuck out his tongue. He dialed the phone and waited for someone to answer while he reexamined the strange faces in the photograph, looking for some connection between them, some resemblance between them and himself.

Your daddy's coming home, kids, he said. Just you wait. We'll have us a good time. Daddy, he thought. When was the last time one of those faces had called him Daddy?

Doreen hadn't answered, even after fifteen rings. Leaving work early, Merrill stopped off on his way home for some flowers and a newspaper with the movie listings. Turning onto his street, he saw a dark blue car pull away from his house. It looked like the same make as Frank's, but Frank should still have been in bed from his accident.

Hi, honey, I'm home, Merrill shouted. Surprise, he said, as Doreen emerged from the kitchen wiping an ashtray dry. She plunked it down on the coffee table.

You're home early, is all she said. She smelled of gin, and Merrill forced himself not to look at his watch.

It's a surprise, he said. He held the flowers behind his back. He smiled. Here, he said.

What're those?

Flowers, he said. For you. Flowers.

What for? Doreen demanded.

No reason. Here. Refusing to be daunted, he shoved the baby carnations at his wife. Why don't you put them in water? he said.

He watched his wife as she padded toward the kitchen. She still resembled the picture on his desk, but like a photograph the resemblance remained in the outline more than in her spirit. Her spirit was older. But then, he was older, too. Maybe spending more time at home would be good for both of them. He had always dreamed that when he retired, he and Doreen could grow old together. Merrill remembered the photograph of the Normandy cottage he had clipped from a magazine, years ago. He still kept it, hidden in his jewelry case, and it seemed more possible to him now than ever before.

The back door slammed as Merrill settled back on the sofa and began to flip through the paper for the movie listings. It was his daughter, and he listened with a slight sense of unfamiliarity as she spoke to her mother. They whispered and tap water ran intermittently, but he thought he overheard the name Hank. He heard his daughter ask, What's he doing home? Then the hissing of more water along with more whispers. Merrill felt good. Most daughters ignored their parents from what he knew. His daughter shared secrets with her mother. Rather than mind their whispering, he felt as though the fabric of his family was reaching out from the kitchen and drawing him into complicity with it. He closed his eyes.

His daughter's sudden presence in the room startled him. She was standing just inside the living room, inspecting him warily, cautiously, as a small dog will sniff out a larger dog. Merrill smiled broadly at her, the way he imagined a father ought to smile at his daughter who was, as he could see, becoming a young woman.

Hi, sweetheart, he said.

Hi.

How was your day? he said.

Okay, she said, edging past him. Then, turning her back on him, she darted for the stairs.

Hey, Merrill called. I was thinking. How about all of us going out for pizza and a movie? What do you think? That be okay, just the family—

a pizza and a movie? My treat. The look on his daughter's face made him nervous. He laughed. How about that, huh?

Can't, she said. Got a date. Sorry.

Oh, he said. Who with, Hank? A bedroom door upstairs slammed.

Merrill mixed a batch of martinis and carried the shaker into the kitchen for some ice. Doreen sat at the kitchen table, hunched over a book. As he dropped some ice cubes into the blender, one escaped him and skidded across the floor. Without looking up, Doreen said, Don't make a mess.

He set a drink in front of her and leaned back on his heels and sipped his own, looking around at the polished order of the kitchen, sipping and looking. He began to feel like a pigeon drinking not out of thirst but from lack of anything better to do. He felt out of his territory. Finishing his drink, he poured another. The carnations lay with their stems in the sink full of water. He sat down across from his wife and tapped his fingernails on the table. Doreen looked up and then flipped over the page and went on reading.

So, Merrill said. Got a date with old Hank, huh?

Doreen started. The color left her cheeks. What? she said.

Mimi. She said she's going out tonight. With Hank, I assume. Is he a nice boy?

Jeffrey's a nice boy, if that's who you mean. The kind of boy I hope she'll marry, someday. His parents are well-off. His father owns his own company. Jeff works for him after school.

Marriage? Merrill wondered. How old was Mimi, anyway? He said, And where's Jim-boy and Tommy?

Jim who? his wife said, closing the book on her thumb and looking at him questioningly.

Jim-boy. Jimmy. Our son, for God's sake.

Don't you raise your voice at me, Doreen said. Had she but added "young man," she would have sounded exactly like his mother. His name is James, Doreen went on, not Jim-boy. James. They're in Cato at a basketball game. They're going to stay overnight with my mother.

Oh, Merrill said, disappointed. I thought . . . oh, well, he said, trying to be mild about his disappointment. The best-laid plans, he said under his breath. The web of family seemed to be all around him and yet it didn't include him. He felt a little bitter.

What's the matter now, Merrill? Doreen said.

Nothing, he said. Nothing. He couldn't keep the hurt out of his voice as he added, I just hoped we could spend an evening together for once. You and me. The kids. It seems like I don't know what's going on around here anymore. No one bothers to tell me what they're doing.

Oh, fine, Doreen said. You just come home early one day, having made plans for all of us without asking any of us. Now you're going to act hurt because everyone has already made plans. You know you might know more about what goes on around here if you'd been here more. And now you're going to sit there feeling sorry for yourself like everyone has let you down. Doreen's face flushed red. Jeez, Merrill, she said, jeez. Just who the hell do you think you are?

Nobody, Merrill yelled. Just nobody. A nobody who works day in and day out at a job he hates so you can have a nice house, so his sons can be off anywhere and wherever and his daughter can go out with a nice boy whose father's rich, unlike hers, and maybe even marry Hank or someone like him, which seems to be none too soon for you. A nobody who is married to a Mrs. Nobody Bitch with three nobodies who impersonate children. Merrill raised his hand to strike someone and stopped. Doreen ducked from the room. I'm sick, he shouted. I'm just sick. Fed up. You hear? And I'm going to be around here a lot the next couple of weeks, if that'll make you happy.

Merrill went outside. The cold air stung at first but after a few minutes felt brisk and good. He grabbed the snow shovel one of his sons had left stuck into a bank. He wrenched it loose from the snow, and began knocking the carefully banked snow into the driveway. He worked his way down toward his Buick. He could see the outline of himself in the windshield as he swung the shovel into the grille, denting it. Then he sat himself in the snow and wept.

DOREEN WAS IN THE SHOWER AND MERRILL SAT ON THE EDGE OF THE bed, waiting for her to finish. He wanted to explain. Maybe he could tell her about the way work had been, the way Fedelman seemed to take it for granted that his accountants would sign their names to illicit tax returns. Perhaps he ought to tell her about the madwoman sticking her tongue out at him every morning. He leaned over and methodically tied his shoelaces tighter.

Doreen came out of the bathroom with a mushroom of steam. She went to her vanity table and began brushing her hair, looking at him from time to time in the mirror.

God, Merrill thought, I don't want any of this. Doreen? he said. I'm sorry. I don't want it to be this way.

Doreen stopped brushing, momentarily. Her mouth curled at the corners in a sarcastic smile as though she didn't believe him. As though she wasn't going to believe anything he might say.

Listen, he said. Why don't we go out to dinner, the two of us, and talk? Huh? What do you say? Like old times. Like before.

Before what? Doreen said.

Listen, honey. I'm sorry I blew up. I really am. Look, work has been pretty rough, you know? Lately. I'm all nerves. Strange things have been happening.

Doreen wiggled into a dress and then went into the bathroom again. He could see the shadow of her arm as she stroked lipstick on her lips, and then she came out and began fishing through the closet for a coat.

Stop, Merrill said. Would you just stop a second?

She stood looking at him. He closed his eyes and stretched backward on the bed. Jesus, he said. Jesus.

You know I really care about you, don't you? The kids? Merrill talked, trying to find a place to begin. But listen. These weird things keep happening to me. I don't know what's real or not anymore. For instance, on my way to work? There's been this woman. . . .

I haven't got time for true confessions, Merrill, Doreen said, striding toward the door.

No, Merrill said. It's not like that. This woman. . . .

Doreen turned on him. Look, Merrill, she said. We can make this simple. Let's just say the oysters haven't worked for us and leave it at that. You've been having an affair. Okay. We've both been having affairs. It's time that got out in the open. But there are the kids to think about, so now we've got to decide what we're going to do and how. Okay, Merrill? You think about it and decide. I'll leave it up to you.

ONCE HIS MIND STOPPED RACING, MERRILL THOUGHT ABOUT IT AND HE found the decision the easiest thing in the world. He showered, dressed, drove carefully down to the office and collected some papers, and then drove home. Home, he thought. It was odd that he felt for the first time in years that he knew, really knew, where he was.

Working on the dining room table, he stood up every half hour and either went to the kitchen for a glass of water or stretched in the middle of the room, marching in place, lifting his knees up as high as he could, with his chin held up and out. Once he climbed the stairs and lifted the advertisement for his Normandy cottage from its hiding place in his jewelry case. He carried it downstairs, looking at it as though it were not a dream cottage but only an ad, and then watched the flames tinge green and blue from the dyes as it shriveled in the fireplace.

By the time he heard Mimi come home, he had nearly finished revising the tabulations on the Stavros account. He felt expectant, almost happy. He would go to work Monday and set the folder on Fedelman's desk. So what if several thousands claimed as business expenses were really payments on a house for a woman Stavros was known to visit on weekends. Everyone, after all, did those things. When he finished, Merrill climbed the stairs staunchly, pausing in front of his daughter's bedroom door, where he stood with his hands opening and closing as they hung from his arms, before he decided not to disturb her and went to get into his own bed.

He curled up in bed and clasped a pillow in his arms. It felt soft and good. By the time Doreen came in, turned on the dim light beside her bed, and began to slip out of her clothes, Merrill was long lost in sleep, happily figuring up his dreams in columns.

Interlude

I.

GERTRUDE WAS AN OLD WOMAN AND EXCEPT FOR THE OCCASION NEVER would have made the trip from McMinnville to California, since she had been there only the year before and each time she came she privately promised herself the luxury in the future of remaining at home. The furniture had made the decision for her—the bureau, mainly, which wore the Carrara marble topping that blankly reminded her of her past and her future and which, though she laughed at it, covered it, threatened to sell it, stolidly won out in the end. So Gertrude McMinn had retrieved her travel case from the attic and packed a red wool suit and the heavy black shoes that limped from use, a book of Greek poems, a novel, and her brief notes on the flowering eucalyptus; canceled her piano lessons, phoned her minister, and postponed her lecture to the dwindling botanical club; and on the late flight into San Francisco, had adjusted her attitude—or, more precisely, had prepared to suspend it.

Startled by the morning's light, she opened one eye and let it range over the unfamiliar room in an attempt to discover even the most random ordering of the clutter. She bit her lip. She knew her one eye was a trick, a tasteless pretense of hoping she was not there. "It continues," Gertrude said to herself. She rose from bed and tripped the shades, letting them snap into contracted mute rolls at the top of the windows' casements. "Zoe." The Greek made her laugh. It made "life" sound so cheerful and she used the word as a solitary thrush uses song to scatter the omens of gale. It kept her connected with the past when she felt, as she did safariing barefooted through the cluttered room, detached, discarded by the future into the linoleum-veneered catchall room of a one-story suburban house. Outside a bird cried, "Zoh-EE, zoh-EE," as if in answer to her, answered in its turn by a hidden frog.

She might have used a species of bird to argue against the human habit of singular ceremony. Some birds battled their mates annually in a regenerative process of identification and trust. But humans performed their ceremony once—one moment cast by tremors of intent and forged in the realization, This, this is my husband, till death or lawyers do us part. From that moment extended the tabula rasa, the sheet of marble to be etched by pressures of indifference and interdependence. As a musician, Gertrude had no natural objection to marriage. All she ever wanted to control was her own experience of her granddaughter's wedding, a performance she continued secretly to dread, as one dreads a high school performance of Wagner.

"Zoh-EE," twirped the bird.

"Bugs," said the frog.

Gertrude gazed out the window, searching for some sign of the clouds that had chased her plane south from Corvallis. The sky was empty. The weather would be effusively mild. "It's a shame," she said, "the way nature mimics." The early morning breeze flushed the bird with a last staccato chirrup from the great ginkgo in the front yard as the preternatural silence of the house was broken by the rush of toilet water through the labyrinth of pipes plumbed, she thought, to the sea. Slowly now, the house would come alive, tugging its masons from their labors of the night and excavating them from their rooms. Then the noise would proliferate, massing together a colloquy of preparations arguing toward the granite calm of the culminating ceremony. From the densest layers of her mind compressed by time beyond time, from a region of memory that did not exist, sprang the words, "from stone we came, to stone we shall return." Realizing she had spoken these, she listened for the bird and the frog, but neither replied. "This was silly," she decided. "These words." She attempted to will herself back into her book. But unlike the bird ("Zoh-EE," she thought), she was unable to escape the veined patina of the day.

The occasion, then: her granddaughter Marie's wedding a gardener from the Benevolent Association's hospital in San Francisco. Marie. Shy, sweet, plump. "How she's lost weight for this day," Gertrude thought. After years of proficiency in the language of love and existential philosophy Marie had decided, or acquiesced, after due deliberation, to bestow her favors on this lawn mower from Oklahoma ("Oh-kay-el-ay-aytch-oh-em-ay," Gertrude sang)—the favors comprising a sugared assortment of pies, cakes, and cookies and the deliberations consisting mainly of the infrequency, the dearth in fact, of offers. It was this dearth that made the occasion a relief to Marie's mother, Donna. Donna desired from life only the weddings of her four daughters, Vicki, Marie, Stella, and Pam, as though reproduction justified her own mistake.

Relief in this house was solemn, expressed in the methodical preparations redundantly coursing over the previous year. "How could it be otherwise," thought Gertrude, "when the gown's original purchaser—Marie's Aunt Helen, the primum mobile of the gown's short history—had died inconsiderately last year on the eve of Stella's wedding?" Relief: as if the whole house sighed over its second mortgage. Solemn: as if the people contained by the walls of the house resisted the word for her daughter-in-law's metabolic illness. Gertrude resented this latter as much as she resented her family's avoidance of what some of them believed of her.

"But Marie is not ugly!" Gertrude exclaimed to the hide-a-bed as it transformed into an uneasy sofa. "Neither is she unattractive." She punched the third cushion into place. Marie was like a well-sodded lawn: The grooming, the shrubbery, an unusual shape perhaps, could make all the difference, could cause someone (a stranger even) approaching the main house to notice and even remark upon the lawn.

("Your garden is marvelous, the lawn so richly green, inviting," she heard her bureau say. "Thank you, Eighteenth Century," Gertrude replied, graciously nodding her head.)

They thought she was odd, speaking as she did with her furniture.

("The shrubs . . . over there," the bureau pointed, "are new?")

She thought it was odd that their furniture did not talk back. But then their furniture was new and there was no understanding, none expressed at least, between them and their furnishings.

("Yes. Just in last week. The lawn, of course, is like an old friend. Perhaps we will dine with it.")

Gertrude laughed, imagining the scene.

"An old friend." She wagged her finger at the headless gown ensconced in the corner as though it had sneered, irritated by her momentary lapse of attitude. For besides being her granddaughter, Marie was also a friend whom she had often thought about and wished better for. "What if you had not won?" she challenged the gown. Perhaps then Marie would have done more with her life, become a linguist perhaps instead of giving it all up and cooking and cleaning, passing time until she was buried. Gertrude finished fixing her hair in a bun, solemnly suspended just above the nape of her neck.

"Zoh-EE." From the window, the bird was hidden. All she could see to confirm its return was a faint movement of leaves among the boughs. "Habit," she called to the bird as though invoking its winged attitude.

"Mother?" There was a minutely perceptible tapping at her door. Had her son overheard her? "Mother, it's time to get up." Lyle's voice behind the door sounded even and smooth, muffled like granite clothed in dust, vaguely reminiscent of her grandfather's stonecutter's voice from long before and far away, gentle but strong.

"I'll be there shortly," she said, as brightly as she could.

Putting on the shoes that limped, she felt sorry, as she had felt sorry when her grandfather told her over and over as he'd grown old that the real danger in cutting stone was that weak spots might develop and the massive blocks shatter, worthless, along a single fissure. "This remember you," he had repeated over and over. "This remember you."

Behind her she heard a smirk, or thought she heard one, from the gown's corner. "I am not senile," she exclaimed. The all-too-familiar gown, worn last year by Stella as years before it had been worn by Stella's mother, the gown which had seen action time and time before, stood there stolidly like a columnar candle still smoking though cold. Everything, in the moment of their staring at each other, seemed compressed into the lacy threads of the white taffeta dress, the human beings who each had stretched its threads little more than the members of a Greek chorus. "Well," she laughed into the mirror, adjusting her brooch, "I suppose if someone can't keep the closet doors shut upon it, then one must simply hope that after the actors depart the chorus will stream on stage chanting Joy instead of Woe."

"Zoh-EE. Zoh-EE," trilled the bird, as Gertrude emerged beaming for breakfast.

II.

GERTRUDE WAS BOTH EXCITED AND IRRITATED TO SEE VICKI AS SHE crossed from the newly appended guest room toward what once had been the back door, until Pam had been conceived on one of those twilight let's-make-it-right vacations which often produces that solitary child who stands apart eight or ten years from the first several. Walking on the outer edge of the left shoe, which promised to separate from the sole beneath the big toe, she found her granddaughters preparing breakfast in the kitchen. Vicki danced swiftly to and from the drawers of silverware. Marie and Stella moved silently, almost methodically, avoiding brushing or bumping each other in the rectangularly narrow kitchen. The youngest, Pam, was planted on a barstool at the counter separating the kitchen and dining room, rolling balls of butter and languidly placing them on the tip of her tongue, which slid in with the butter balls, then out, empty. Gertrude paused on the doorsill, surveying the scene of family industry, and concentrated on not limping duck-footed into the room.

On the wall behind Vicki were several clocks—a Swiss cuckoo, a Japanese centrifugal, a Big Ben from Westinghouse. Against the ocher wall rested the grandfather clock, the one her own late husband had cherished for fifty years. Gertrude laughed. There was in her late husband's buying and selling of clocks something that amused her, some relationship to this weekend that eluded her in a mist of humor. Of the clocks on the wall, only Big Ben seemed to be functioning.

"Good morning, Grandmother," Stella said, echoed immediately by Marie.

"Hi, Grandma." Vicki came over to kiss her. "Did you sleep well?"

"Good morning." Gertrude smiled and, observing the disappearance of another butter ball, replied, "I did. A beautiful morning outside, isn't it?"

Marie leaned across the sink to look outside as her father, Lyle, slipped in from the hall, wishing his mother and daughters a good day.

To one not related to the family, it would seem that this was a usual family breakfast on a Saturday morning in September, with the usual duties and responsibilities of the day assessed and accepted. What was unusual was the presence of the entire McMinn family: the four granddaughters, Gertrude, and her son, Lyle. "Donna will be out shortly, Mother," Lyle murmured to Gertrude. No one else said anything.

Feeling the compressed silence, Gertrude began to miss her bureau. This room seemed a disused attic strung with the cobwebs of what was never said. One had to move carefully or not at all if one were not to

become entangled in the emotions drifting this way and that on the currents of air—currents so imperceptible that they were identifiable only
by the drift and curve of the filaments—and balancing to indifference.
Vicki alone made happy noises while she ate. Marie seemed still to be
watching out the window. Stella's flushed cheeks quivered as she stared
down at her plate, disoriented by this day which was duplicating her
own wedding day, thinking, "A year's time has passed." Pam slouched at
the far end near her father and Gertrude was surprised to notice the
prettiness showing through in spite of the butter balls. "Not that prettiness will make any difference," Gertrude told herself. Yet one might reasonably expect a difference to be made. "But then. . . ." Gertrude lurched
to a halt, touching her brooch to be certain it was situated properly.

She wished to say something to sweep the cobwebs from the room,
to draw out the words floating in the silence. She glanced from head to
hung head, one by one, not discouraged but concerned—no, worried—
that the intrusion of thought might send Marie skittering out the window or cause Stella to collapse into the sunny-side of her eggs. In
frustration she asked Lyle, how was his new job?

"It's okay."

"Zoh-EE." Gertrude's eyes darted from crown to crown of the lowered heads of her granddaughters. She heard a bureau drawer slam shut,
a door open.

"The people are real nice. They keep me busy."

"Lovable Lyle, they call him." Donna's laugh howled down the hall.
The sighing knives and clicking forks seemed to obey the abrupt force
that had stopped the clocks on the wall.

"H-e-e-e-r-e's Mother," Vicki whispered in mock introduction. She
received the tick of a warning look from Stella.

"They call up here and ask if Lovable is home. I call him Dummy.
Hey, Dummy, I yell, are you home?" As Donna entered, her voice rocked
out over the table. Stella blushed as she examined the particles of food
on her plate. Marie concentrated on the window, attempting to complete

her immaculate decoding of the Sanskrit weather. Vicki sighed. Gertrude covered her gaping mouth, staring at Donna, who walked on legs like Chartres' steeples, inverted, her gray flaccid skin veined like an ivied tower.

"Hey, Dummy, she calls me." Lyle uttered a laugh not false, not yet hollowed of meaning. He seemed embarrassed by the attention forced upon him.

"Morning, Gertie. How was your flight?" Donna said.

Gertrude hid her expression behind her napkin.

("Gertie!" the bureau exclaimed.)

"Fine," she answered as she and Donna looked blankly at each other.

("So this is what a year can do," her bureau whispered.)

Gertrude brushed the bureau away with her hand as one brushes off the annoyance of a fly just after it has scratched together its hind legs and flown.

Donna ignored this sign of Gertrude's aging. "Pam, damn it, don't slump like that!" she said, her breath blasting stale odor into Gertrude's face. Turning away to gasp gently for air, Gertrude saw Vicki's fork jam hard into the ham on her plate.

(The bureau remarked that Donna's skin looked more like damp papier-mâché than the gray stone of a tower. "As though," it hinted, "one could peel away one limp strip at a time without altering the shape until the final layer revealed amorphous wads of crumpled stuffing." Go away! Gertrude ordered the bureau.)

"You'd think today was a funeral. Marie, you should be glad some-one is marrying you. . . ."

Stella stared more intently, if that was possible, at her breakfast. Gertrude wished she might be in that plate staring back at the blushing Stella, imagining her purpose as on a cloudy night one imagines the pur-pose of a solitary star peeping through the portents of storm. Vicki's mouth opened as she twisted the tines of her fork in the fat-veined sinews of the ham, and then clamped shut like a rusty trap. Gertrude nervously straightened her brooch as she glanced beyond the slumping Pam to her son whom, because of the light piercing through the windows, she could not see clearly. No one moved. No one except Donna, whose blood-veined eyes glowed dimly as her small mouth chiseled away at the indifference of her family.

The grandfather clock whirred, clicked, tripped an interior mechanism, then tolled. Gertrude counted five tolls in all, which she knew was wrong even before she finished. One always missed the first few tolls of unexpected bells. One's mind did not even think to begin counting them until after the second or third note and even then one's mind resisted the slow numbering of the clock, rejected it as silly—her mind saying all through her inaccurate counting, "Simply look at the face of it." None of the wall clocks struck. No housed bird emerged to chorus agreement. As if it were a sign, the family began to rise one by one and slip away, except Donna, who was still eating, and Vicki, who alternately looked at her mother and Gertrude.

Gertrude sat wondering, thinking, "This is how it goes, the generations," and watching her daughter-in-law.

"Zoh-EE," a bird cried in the distance.

"Saint Anne's Foot!" Gertrude laughed out, sharing a joke with Donna. It was one of her and Vicki's private stock, which in the process of aging had fermented into a password for which only the bouquet and the color remained. She sat beaming at Donna. But Donna, concerned about the time and what was yet to be done to complete the occasion, did not look up.

"If I ever get married," Vicki exclaimed, "it will be in an orange sari."

III.

GERTRUDE FELT MISPLACED IN HER RED WOOL SUIT, WHICH WAS BEGINning to wrinkle, and her shoes, which fairly hobbled with pain. She was exhausted. She had watched Donna race about carping, cajoling, pleading, and threatening. She'd ridden back and forth and back with her son in the car to fetch forgotten stockings, a toothbrush, the veil. She'd met Mesdames, Messrs., Misses, and a Ms. At last, she'd been seated next to an elegant silver-haired woman who was dressed in an Oriental dress of bright Polynesian colors, whose name she had just forgotten. In her mind, Gertrude simply called the woman Peacock and avoided using her name by calling her "you" or touching her arm to gain her attention. Though inconvenient in one way, this namelessness lent an aura of interest to the memories and family anecdotes Peacock told, made them a puzzle of which Gertrude recognized only a few of the more obvious border pieces.

Across the aisle sat the Oklahomans who, since neither Gertrude nor Peacock had ever met real, actual natives before, were the objects of their circumspect curiosity. They were certainly a large people, amassed in a stolid block ranging from The Rock down to Traffic Light, the only two with any color. Traffic Light was beautiful beneath the rouge and green eye shadow. The Rock, with clumsy prestidigitation, managed to keep her ring finger in view of everyone, and the reflected brilliance of the light emanating from her hand made her seem a Diogenes to the gathering somber witnesses mounting an argument for gray in the pews behind her. By contrast to the groom's guests, the bride's guests were actually colorful, though motley. The bride's mother, who had been disappearing into bathrooms and closets all morning long, reappeared for the last time, seeming remarkably well composed.

With the help of her bureau, Gertrude surveyed all of this with genuine pleasure and never once worried why the names of these people slipped through the sieve of her memory like dust. She knew why. Or at least she had definite suspicions why, which the bureau confirmed.

The sanctuary was large and hot, the ceremony delayed just late enough to allow the heat of the people present to pack down around them in the nave. The organist, sepulchral and white-faced like a man who's spent his life darkly underground, looked to be dozing.

"Perhaps we all have perished," Gertrude whispered, "and this is forever."

"What?" asked Peacock.

Gertrude smiled and shook her head, fingering her brooch. She longed to have the whole odd affair done and finished right then, condensing the dirge of the wedding march into a few moments of living cacophony. A massive door opened at the side of the apse, an anonymous man stepped through, and the door closed with a muffled, reverberating echo.

"That's an exquisite brooch," Peacock said.

("He's perfect!" the bureau exclaimed.)

"Thank you," Gertrude said. He was, indeed. This minister—or whatever they called him in the Mary Eddy of their religion—seemed the ideal person to join these two families together irrevocably and irreparably.

"I used to talk to myself," Peacock said. "Especially last year when my last remaining daughter passed away."

Gertrude was about to declare that she had been talking not to herself but to her marble-topped bureau. She was relieved to find herself saved from that mistake by the Grand Puppeteer (the bureau's name for Her), who suddenly lifted the stiff arms of the organist, stood the guests on their feet, and exacted final adjustments in the position and stance of the anonymous minister. Then the minister's eyes slowly lifted on the distance as the motleys' somber eyes turned inward and back toward the same empty place in idealized space.

Donna teetered on her steeples and Gertrude's head swam as their eyes joined the others. A film formed over Gertrude's vision—as happened when she was too long in a department store or aquarium and she began to feel assaulted by the overwhelming crowd of things or animals. As she looked, it seemed she looked—lighted by the light of The Rock—beyond any memory down all eternity. Stoically, she observed the gown slowly, in step to the time created by human beings for the occasion, move up the aisle into one shattered heap of the present. Patiently, now, their attitudes suspended by their individual devices and holding them aloof, Gertrude and Donna watched.

"I do," the bride said, and the motleys began to cough and choke.

"I do," said the groom, met with somber coughing.

"I now pronounce you . . . ," the minister said without intonation, and the halves of the church were conjoined in coughing, choking, and the rustling of handkerchiefs, interrupted only by the correction of the ring from the groom's right hand to his left. Gertrude and Donna smiled.

IV.

DOWN THE TADPOLE FELT THE LONG GRAY-GLOVED FINGERS OF A TALL gaunt woman with white hair. A blue tadpole with one eggshell eye— that was the reception line, weighted at the head by the gown, bulging into a bulk of blue bridesmaids, then thinning into a spotted tail, tipped red. ("Look at her shoes," someone said. But Gertrude did not mind; she was beginning to grin uncontrollably, her brooch tilting, ready to dive into the declivity of her bosom.) After pausing to peck the tadpole's eye with lips and gloves, the woman moved down the line, at random intervals causing the body to ripple with animation until she reached the grinning Gertrude, whose hands felt the gray caress of the woman's fingers.

"You must be Lyle's mother," the woman said evenly.

"Yes," Gertrude smiled. "And who are you?"

"I'm a reader."

"I love to read!" The patina, rubbed by the day's erosion, brightened her features. "Why just this morning I was reading Honor Tracy . . . a rather nice Irish wit . . . do you know her?"

"No, no, my dear. *In* the church," the woman said.

That was an odd confession, Gertrude thought, as she continued smiling and passed Gaunt Gloves into the room.

Gradually, inevitably, the ripples subsided as the room filled with chatter, smiles, introductions. The tadpole's body began to disintegrate, merging with the muted colors of the room. Gertrude removed herself to a wall lined with folding chairs and watched, alternately happy at the confused activity and then imagining herself at home, the interruption of this fifth act of her life over and the play resumed. The room filled with faceted glints of light and color as she observed The Rock sidling about from circle to circle with her left hand raised. Traffic Light stood, blushing then winking, flirting with the constant sequence of young men.

The cake was cut and dribbled from forks onto plates. Donna disappeared and then returned. Spotting Gertrude grinning alone ("Just look at her dowdy red suit," someone nodded toward the wall), she crossed to her and sat down. "Well, Gertie," she sighed, fumbling in her purse. "A mint?" Gertrude, who did not care for candy, accepted one. "Well," Donna rambled on, her words indistinct like the colors in the room, "this is a happy day. Last year, you know, I had to sit through Stella's wedding knowing that Helen . . . the night before, and Stella, who didn't know, in her gown . . . Helen had. . . ."

"Died?" Gertrude said.

"Popped off," Donna blurted.

Yes, Gertrude thought. Yes, Donna is drunk, nearly slobbering.

"Oh, they're all so. . . . It's all so . . . ," Donna said. A strange pride emanated from Donna through Gertrude and out into the room where it hovered above the compressed layers of guests.

The wedding meats were served and snapped up as though by crocodiles. A blood-red punch was seriously sipped from plastic cups. Donna ceased leaving the room and sat pouring vodka from a flask into her plastic tumbler. Gertrude watched and watched and watched, grinning the while.

"Mother," Lyle whispered. "It's time to go home."

"Yes." Gertrude laughed and, pulling Donna to her steeples, walked her from the room.

V.

THE GOWN WAS UNPINNED AND PLACED, TEMPORARILY, ON THE DRESS form. The couple, with tendrils of "we" beginning to transmute former evanescence into veined solidity, was riced away on their three-day honeymoon. Back in her room, alone, the door shut on the no-longer-sighing house, Gertrude stood laughing at the gown, remembering the year Vicki was nine and they had gone Christmas shopping together in San Francisco. Amid the bustle and crunch of the crowd they had spotted, solitarily occupying a large department store window, a richly jeweled case containing, according to the sign, *The Relic of Saint Anne's Foot.*

"What's that mean, Grandma?" Vicki had inquired with all the seriousness of her age.

"'Saint Anne's Foot'? Why, it means . . . it means names . . . the past . . . doesn't mean anything anymore," Gertrude had said, trying not to laugh.

In the afterglow of The Rock, Gertrude saw her own solitude. It was a right that had no age and for which she had longed for so long—the right to refuse, to not succumb to the debt of the past but instead to become the past, to be happy in the serenity of no promised tomorrows in spite of the somber, woeful arguments of gray.

Gertrude remembered her grandfather's words of long ago and far away, and here, now, she resolved to forget what he had said about the dangers of cutting stone. Before she slept, she was wishing that if Vicki ever did get married, it would be in an orange sari; that the wedding would be barefoot on the beach at Big Sur; and that the groom would be somehow different, a black man perhaps, from the southern tip of Africa, or a Lebanese Jew who had never, not in the deepest part of his imagination, not for a moment, dreamed of cutting stone.

As she lay in bed, she listened. All she heard was the fine warm drizzle of rain on the tree and roof, and the gentle croak of a frog. The bird had succumbed to habit and flown.

Fog

CARLA SAID THAT HARTMAN DIDN'T LOVE ANYONE. THAT WASN'T TRUE, Hartman said. Not true at all. What did she mean? He preferred women to men.

Carla said maybe he couldn't love anyone—at least that was what she was beginning to think. Maybe it was because of his race.

I've had a bad year, Hartman said. It was true: His mother's early death dated the opening of what he called his bad year. His brother had killed himself. Hartman had seen that death coming, he decided when he looked back on it. But had he done enough to prevent it? His grandmother's heart, pickled in Mad Dog, had given out. And to top it all off, his sister had run off with a Papuan from New Guinea. A missionary, to boot.

Each event was caused by a weak heart. That's what he decided. It seemed to run in his family. Hartman worried about what that meant for him.

Excuses, Carla had said. Your bad year has lasted nearly two. When's it going to stop, Hartman?

That had made Hartman angry. She hadn't had such awful things. She didn't know. Did she expect him to go around smiling and acting happy when he wasn't?

No, Carla had said.

Had Carla given him a reason, he could have accepted her walking out on him. But she hadn't, not really, and the scene kept coming back to him in all its abruptness, like a change in seasons. Carla had just left, quietly packed all her clothes and left. Moved out. Hadn't she said anything else?

Hartman was left alone.

All night a bewildered tomcat had made the neighborhood aware of the longing he felt, and Hartman, unable to sleep, sat up reading magazines he had purchased in the drugstore near where he worked. In some of the magazines were foldouts of women and he would stop and ponder them with indifference, wondering why he didn't feel more, and then go on reading. While he read, a cold front pushed into the valley, bundling southward. The tulle fog outside made everything wet and blind.

Carla was a commentator on a local news program which Hartman watched every morning without fail. He turned the sound off and spoke to her. Today the picture kept edging up as if it would roll, and then settled back and became still. He opened a book and tried to read. Now and then, he glanced up to catch the picture fluttering. He saw Carla smile secretly at the weatherman with the pointer, before the camera switched to a clear outline of New York State with what looked like cotton candy pulling across it. Her smile must mean something, he thought, but he didn't want to know what.

The camera switched back and he stared at Carla's lips. He thought he liked her better like this. She had a hoarse, mechanical voice—he couldn't forget it, like the memory of a dentist's drill—and she turned her head quickly toward the red "ON" light as it jumped from camera to camera. She smiled. She knew he was watching. He could tell.

Hartman wished he could direct the cameras, cutting from one shot to the next so fast that her smile would freeze as her head spun on its neck.

He laid the book open on the edge of the bed, listening to the binding crack, and tried to sleep. A dull ache seemed to travel from joint to joint in his body, disappearing from his right knee as he gave himself up to the rutted vee of the old mattress and as suddenly reappearing in his elbow. It went to his shoulder near his heart making him wonder what a heart attack must feel like and if he was having one. But it was only his right shoulder, and he knew where heart attacks started.

Still, he got up and went to the bathroom, gobbled a handful of aspirin, and stood absently before the medicine cabinet. The shelves seemed half-empty to him, a bit messy. Everything was there, though. The mirror showed him a man who was a bit haggard, and Hartman made a face at him, pulling back his ears and clenching his jaw. Teeth okay; a little stained by the nicotine of his long talks with Carla, but sound. He tapped a cigarette from the pack beside the sink, lit it watching himself, then grabbed at the flesh around his waist and snapped the band of his briefs with his thumb. Carla had bought him dozens of bikini briefs in flamboyant colors, and he continued to wear them even though they embarrassed him when he undressed at the gym.

Back on the bed, he ignored the ache in his stomach and imagined flirting with the cashier at the drive-in Burger Boy near his apartment. She was probably in high school. His flirting with her was only harmless fun, and besides, if she were a few years older—four, say—it'd be okay. Why should four years make such a difference?

"Been known to happen," he said.

He imagined her there, crushed by the slope of the mattress against him. He stroked her hair as it fell across his shoulder and the ache in his stomach ceased. The thought that she probably cared about hot cars and suntans and boys that he called ridge-bellied roundheads hovered for a moment around the outside of his mind.

Hartman woke up with the feeling that someone had been there with him. Her face was blurred, so he wasn't certain who. Wouldn't have been his wife. Of the women he knew, Peggy's home office had moved to Boston, and she'd gone with the office. Jill he hadn't heard from since she called to say she was broke and he had mailed her two 20-dollar bills. She hadn't called again.

The phone was ringing. "Yeah? Hartman here."

"Hi," the voice on the other end said, tentative.

"Oh, hi, Teri, what's up?"

"I called to see how you were." There was a long pause.

"Fine," Hartman said, at last. "I'm fine."

"You broke your promise again."

"Yeah, well . . . I know."

"It's weird to go to sleep with someone and wake up to find him gone, you know, Hartman? It's like you think it's criminal."

He didn't know what to say. Did he care?

"As if," he said, for loss of anything better.

"What?"

"Never mind. Listen, you want me to come over tonight?"

Another pause. Teri sighed. "Oh, all right. But one condition. You go to sleep here, you wake up here, too. I mean it. Otherwise we're finished. I really mean it, Hartman. Done. Kaput. Deal?"

"See you tonight," he said. He hung up.

He closed his eyes in the shower as he lathered and tried to see the drive-in cashier clearly in his imagination. It was no use. Carla's face from the television kept pushing it out of his mind.

"Bitch!" he said. She had always been like that, his wife, like a mommy keeping him close to her, watching his every move, making him confess whatever he might be thinking.

Teri, on the other hand, told him everything *she* might be thinking.

He had met her in the canteen in the basement of the building he worked in. She'd been sitting at a table near him and while he was eating his roast beef sandwich, he overheard her friend ask Teri if she'd been to any good movies lately. They decided to go to one together. Hartman had lent them a newspaper to look at the movie listings, and then rashly offered to take them. It turned out when he showed up at her door that night that only Teri could go. Something had come up for her roommate.

Still disturbed by the medicine cabinet as he dried himself off, he went into the bedroom and poured out a neat bourbon from the bottle on the nightstand. He sipped it as he got dressed. "Nothing wrong with Teri," he said as he tucked himself into neon blue bikini briefs. Athletically trim. Kind. A little boring; like a newspaper column, she was all event and no meat. But then what did he expect, anyway? Only thing Teri ever complained about was his getting dressed and sneaking out of her house in the middle of the night. She had trouble accepting that he couldn't stay. Why, he wasn't sure. But he felt driven to be home before the sun came up. Driven by what? Maybe it was the way Teri seemed to take her pleasure with him as though lust and love were the same thing. Maybe it was habit. Morning light was different, strange, and he liked to be alone in it without having to hear another person's voice.

It was noon and still the thick, low-lying fog made everything eerie and distant as he drove over to the drive-in Burger Boy. He decided to ask the girl how old she was. What did it matter? Why should it matter, anyway? At Hartman's age, which wasn't very old, a girl's skin began to loosen as if the outlines of her body were shifting. Up close, her skin sometimes looked flaky like the crust of a dried-up old lake. And you couldn't tell what would collapse without the support of clothes; just watching a girl his age undress was suspenseful and a little frightening.

He'd been lucky, though. Peggy, then Jill; and Teri wasn't bad. He remembered how on their first date she had suggested he spend the night with her as he put on his jacket to go home. She had smiled nakedly at him when he asked her if she wasn't going to turn out the light before he undressed, and said, "However you need it." Her face was plain, but her skin seemed young. Afterward, he was shaken by the fact that he felt nothing, nothing at all. "Uh-huh," she'd said as he'd tried to get dressed. She'd pushed him back down and taken her pleasure with him again. And again.

Hartman rolled down his driver's window and leaned out toward the speaker embedded in the fiberglass smile of a gaily painted Burger Boy. It looked like a fat homosexual dressed for the circus. An arm emerged from the service window and handed a bag to the car in front of him. The car pulled out and around, and parked in the lot. Its taillights flashed and went out.

"Can I help you?"

"Maybe," he said. "Depends on how old you are."

"Okay, buddy . . . ," the Burger Boy began.

"It's me," he said. "Hartman." He watched the mirror tilted outside the service window in which she could see the cars. Could she recognize his car in all this fog?

"I'm old enough, Hartee." The Burger Boy emitted a giggle and went dead for a moment.

"Hey, what's your name, anyway?"

"Janet," the Burger Boy replied after taking a minute to think it over.

"Okay, Janet, I'll have a double cheese, onion rings, and a Coke."

"Pepsi okay?"

"Pepsi."

"That's a double cheese, onion rings, and small or large Pepsi?"

"Large," he said. Before the speaker went dead again he acted on impulse. "Say, Janet, what time do you get off?"

"Who's asking?"

"Hartman. Hartman," he repeated, regretting his impulsiveness. But he felt that it was too late now to turn back.

"Right. Hartee. Why are you asking?"

"Well," he said, feeling snared. Trapped by his own decision. "I was thinking you might like to go out sometime."

The Burger Boy speaker went dead again. Longer, this time, than usual, and Hartman hoped he hadn't gotten her in trouble. The car behind him honked and he was forced to move up to the window.

"I'm serious!" he yelled at Burger Boy. "I mean it."

He paid Janet and accepted the bag of food. He felt depressed, now, but obliged to go through with it. "Well?" he asked.

Janet seemed to be laughing; she cupped her hand over her mouth. With her free hand she pointed at the bag. "6 P.M." was written on it in black grease pencil. As he drove home he thought, "I'll be damned," and then he recalled that he'd forgotten to ask how old she really was.

Hartman forgot about feeling snared. He felt almost hopeful as he ran his Saturday errands. At the food co-op they'd hired a new checker and he stood in her line. The other line cleared through faster, of course. He tried not to mind.

"Hi," he offered as she began ringing up his items. "You're new here," he said when she didn't say anything. "I come here all the time. I'm a regular."

She didn't look up but frowned, concentrating on the unfamiliar keys of the cash register.

"That's good yogurt," he said, watching her punch in 55 cents times seven. "The fruit's at the bottom. You don't even know it's there when you open it. You can eat some of it plain and then you can stir it up a little and get a load of fruit on top of the tart. I like that," he said.

She glanced at him out of the corner of her eye and kept right on checking items through.

"Yes, I like that," he said, as though musing.

The girl paused to shove the accumulated groceries down to the stainless-steel table at the end of the conveyor belt. "Sugar hype," she said.

"Sugar?"

"Too much sugar," she said. He picked up a strawberry yogurt and read the label. "No artificial anything," the label read. But she was right. There was sugar listed under ingredients. Wasn't sugar natural?

"Whoops," he said. "That's one-thirty-nine, not two-ninety-eight. See, here. You punched in the price per pound." She looked disdainfully at where he pointed on the package. "It's one-thirty-nine."

"Carcinogens," she muttered as she made the correction.

Hartman was about to ask, carcinogens? when he heard a familiar voice behind him.

"He giving you any trouble, Rene?"

He turned and saw Carla standing there, shaking her head and smiling. But not the way she did on TV, he noted.

"Hello, Hartman," she said. From the way she said it, she was plainly amused.

"Carla," he said.

"No more than any man," the checker said.

Hartman nervously began to bag his own groceries while Carla stood there watching him, grinning at him whenever he looked at her. He hustled his two bags of groceries toward the door. But Carla, buying a small packet of spice, quickly paid for it and came up beside him at the door.

"Pretty, isn't she?" Carla said.

"Who?" he asked, feigning ignorance.

"Rene. The checker. You were about to make an ass out of yourself, hon." Carla didn't say this angrily or accusingly. She just said it. "How've you been, Hartman?"

"Couldn't be better," he said. He wished she would go away, leave him alone, but she was parked beside him.

"Your love life okay?"

"Couldn't be better," he said again. "Busy all the time." He knew she knew he was lying.

"Listen, if you get lonely, need to talk or tell someone your troubles, you can stop by, you know. Just phone first. In case I have company."

"Thanks," he said, trying to get his car door open with two grocery bags in his arms. Carla took his key and unlocked the door and opened it for him. He practically threw his groceries across into the passenger's seat and climbed in behind the wheel.

"By the way, Hartman," Carla said. The laugh was back in her voice. "Save yourself the bother with Rene."

Hartman looked up at her innocently, trying to convince her that she was wrong and he wasn't curious about Rene.

"Let's just say she's not your type," Carla said, and shut his door.

His hopeful mood spoiled, Hartman put away the groceries and then went out to the flower shop where he bought several bouquets and drove out to Morningside Cemetery. He put half of the flowers on his mother's grave and half on his brother's, the way he'd been doing every week for almost two years. He still couldn't get over it. He had cried when his mother died because he didn't feel anything. But with his brother's death it had been different. He wished it'd been him, not his brother who had died, and he cried because of the loss and because of the waste. His grandmother had been shipped to Idaho, to the Lapwai reservation, her ashes to be scattered in the valley with her husband's.

He got down on his knees and began brushing the leaves and dirt off the stone marker above his brother, and he thought of how his mother had always loved his brother best. He'd known that for years. He didn't blame his mother for it; he loved his brother best, too. Who wouldn't? He'd give anything just to have his brother back, to have someone he could talk to who might understand. He laid his cheek against his brother's slab and listened. Joggers crunched up the lane past him and Hartman stood and brushed himself off, aware that what he was doing might look pretty strange. The joggers paid him no attention. For a moment Hartman felt queasy as though he were going to throw up, and then he got control of himself and turned to walk back along the gravel lane that wound out of the burial sites. He wanted to blame his mother and his brother for what had happened to him and Carla, and this time he almost felt a rage swell up inside of him at the unjust-ness of it all. Their dying took them from him and destroyed everything he had with Carla. But his rage vanished when he remembered how Carla had smiled at the weatherman on the morning news, and all he felt was a kind of calm sadness which most people would have called simple exhaustion.

The fog had lifted by the late afternoon. He parked beside a hot-looking Pontiac Firebird in the Burger Boy lot. He delayed for a while, thinking about Carla and Teri, and about Janet inside the drive-in. It was only 5:30, so he waited outside in his car in order not to seem too eager. He felt a little stupid as it was, a twenty-six-year-old man here to pick up a girl who was eighteen, nineteen at the most. The Firebird was black and it had an air spoiler, big tires, and one of those scoops on the hood that sucked in air for turbo-charging. Looking at it made him feel dreary, sitting there as darkness settled in along with the fog, the flames sten-ciled on the Firebird's side flickering in the wet light from the headlights of eager drivers turning past the car service window. Someone sat in the passenger seat, but he couldn't tell if it was a man or a woman; like him, the person wasn't eating, just sitting there passing time.

Finally he climbed out of his car and went inside the Burger Boy. Janet was handing out a bag of food to a customer at the car window, so she didn't see him at first. As she turned around he forced himself to smile and he said, "Surprise!"

"Oh," Janet said.

"Betcha didn't think I'd come back," he said. He tried to act happy and expectant.

"No," Janet said. "I didn't. God," she muttered. "Look, Mr. Hartman, I. . . ."

"Hartman."

"What?"

"My first name. Hartman."

"Oh."

"What's the matter? Too old for you?" Hartman asked. "Afraid to take a chance?"

"No. I . . . I'm not off for another fifteen minutes," she replied.

"I'll wait," he said. "Over there."

He picked a spot that seemed out of the way of the mothers and children, the teenagers and college students who dropped in for dinner. He sat at a round fiberglass table with four red toadstool seats and watched the crowd, wondering what toadstools had to do with the Burger Boy theme and feeling as though he didn't fit in. God, he wished he hadn't come, but it was too late for that.

Janet came out of the employee's door early and came over to him. "Listen, Hartman, I should explain," she began before he could think of something witty to say. "I'm sorry. I really am." She put her hand gently on his forearm. "I was only kidding. I thought you knew that. Jeez-us," she said with a tone of real regret, "I thought you were only kidding, too, or I'd never. . . ."

"Got a boyfriend, huh?" Hartman asked. He could feel himself beginning to grin foolishly. She was way too young, he could see that, and he felt silly sitting there in the Burger Boy making her give him reasons why she couldn't go out with him. But he couldn't stop playing this part.

"No, look, Hartman. I don't go out with men."

"What do you mean you don't go out with men," he said. He laughed in disbelief. He felt a twinge of anger that she didn't even have the kindness to give him a real reason like a boyfriend or a father who'd think he was too old. "That's the stupidest thing," he said. He sneered. "What are you . . . ?"

At that moment the door to the Burger Boy opened and a familiar-looking woman wearing a leather bomber's jacket with a brown fur collar came in and looked around. Her hands were shoved deep into the vent pockets and she wore a watch cap, so he couldn't place her at first. He was still laughing, when she walked over to where he sat as though she were going to speak to him. My God! he realized. It was the checker from the food co-op.

"Hi, honey," she said to Janet.

"Rene, this is . . . ," Janet said.

"We've met," Rene said, no love lost from the tone of her voice. "You ready?"

"Let me grab my things." Janet smiled the same complicit smile he'd seen his wife Carla give the weatherman on the news. He stared at Janet, who shrugged apologetically, and then he turned his gaze on Rene. Janet slipped on her coat. Rene just glared at him. Then she broke into a laugh and took Janet's arm and guided her out the door. Rene said something about carcinogens, and they began laughing together as the door swung shut behind them.

Hartman drove slowly back to the graveyard where he kicked over the upright marker at the head of his mother's grave.

At home, he chose to sit on the floor, his back flat against the wall, and consider the past few years. He began to understand that his wife had been right. He understood why she'd had to leave him and why the medicine cabinet seemed so empty to him, and the wall felt necessary and cold against his back. The phone rang in the other room. He stared. The ache in his back jumped to his shoulder and then became general all through his body. He felt as if there was no weather, would not be any weather anymore, except for the fog. He'd missed it. He was alone. He stared.

He thought of his wife and what she could be doing. He thought of calling her. She'd said he could. But she was probably out with the weatherman, smiling complicitly in the fog. He knew what the secret of her smile was and his lack of that secret feeling hovered around him in the house and between him and the women he knew.

In the other room the phone came alive again and rang and rang. He was tempted to answer it this time in case it might be someone important. But who else would be phoning him besides Teri? He couldn't go over to her house, could he? still? That was not love. It was too late for love.

He closed his eyes and tried to picture Teri's face, the telephone receiver clamped to her ear, the plastic mouthpiece dangling below her chin, an impatient, sad look on her face. His eyes got wet as though the fog had slipped in beneath the doors or through the cracks in the windows.

He did manage for some moments to get a picture of a face. It wasn't Teri's, though. Not Janet's, either. It was his wife's. He wanted to speak to her. He opened his mouth. He meant to say "Bitch!" but instead he heard himself begin to howl like a bewildered tomcat as a new and sharper pain traveled up his groin to his heart. He pressed his palms against his eyes and began to rock forward and back against the pain.

The picture in his mind fluttered, held, fluttered. Then it began to scroll upward faster and faster as he tried to think of what in the world he should do. He struggled to his feet, the pain like nails holding him down, and opened the front door, intending to walk out. The fog like a crowd of hoarse gray cats pushed him backward into a chair and he sat looking at the open door through which the fog entered, uninvited, before it vanished in the palpitating heat of the room.

Storm Watch

THE WEEK AFTER CHRISTMAS, WE DRAGGED OUT THE TREE, TRAILING silvery snippets of tinsel, to the curb, where an unknown service organization would make its skeleton disappear at an unlikely hour. After the tree, we dragged out Kenny. Perhaps I shouldn't tell this story, but maybe I can keep the tone even, and glaze over the crevices and depressions—the horrors even I do not understand—and yet leave you with the grin of truth.

Is this really me? Silly or not, it is a question I ask the white-capped waves, at night, which seem to rise out of nowhere as I balance on a tilting deck of reasons for what has happened. I ask myself when I am alone—when Dara has taken ill to her cabin and I prowl the corners of this ship—looking for my fear, to face it, overpower it, will it away. From what I understand of the sailors' English, we are skirting a typhoon.

I believe that people have a purpose, and that they are circumscribed by it in certain moments—as the few minutes which passed between my birth and Kenny's that made me the older brother. Sometimes we are sure of it, but there are times in which, when they are over, we cannot detect the correct moment—like a sailor who realizes all at once that he is off course, yet does not know how or when he went wrong and cannot admit it to himself because that would be like admitting certain destruction.

Am I that sailor?

The tree, by the time we got around to dragging it out, was little more than a tapered pole with nipples, teats where the branches had been. It hadn't been an expensive tree—it was part of our faith to be against those sorts of displays. And we had been rushed in the selection of it. It had been a dark night and Bobby, in all his useful clumsiness, had gotten hung up in the barbed-wire fence. The moon hung like a scythe or cradle, and I sat in the back of the van with the tree as Kenny raced us away, muttering, "Everyone is expendable." Perhaps he was right. But Beast, Bobby's Saint Bernard, decided to disagree, and when Bobby did not return by the following day, Beast became downright intractable. If you have ever known an animal who earned her name, you will understand what I mean by intractable: 250 pounds going soft even in her bones on your bed when you were exhausted and just wanted to sleep, or plopping her head in your lap while you were sitting on the low couch, leaning up against you while you begged her to move as the nerves in your leg went to sleep. Beast used these tricks. Sometimes I think Beast knew more than I did. It became apparent that Bobby was not entirely expendable.

I offered to pay Bobby's fine, but Kenny wanted to break him out. "Is it worth it?" I said.

"That's not the point," Kenny said. "This isn't the swim team, you know." We had quit that together; I had only trained all those years to be close to him. But I'd known the point, then. What was it now? "It's worth it if you believe," he said.

In what? I thought.

So Kenny, in neat ratiocination, decided that Bobby must be retrieved from the simians at the zoo—his word for the local jail—and he began Plan D. "D," I knew, meant dynamite—I had seen this plan in action before. Not actually *observed*, mind you: Kenny would disappear on his motorcycle one morning and not return for several days; then he'd enter, dirty and worn, sometimes beaten up, waving a news clipping nonchalantly, like one of those tiny flags children carry in parades.

At first I didn't mind. Everything seemed to belong to the movement. But subtly, gradually—unnoticeably—the clippings began to grow like mushrooms, taking more prominent positions in the newspapers.

I know you don't believe it. I don't blame you. Neither had I believed it, and thus it took me a full year before I began to sense that coincidence played an increasingly smaller role. And then came the predictions—a high-voltage power line would be blown up. And sure enough, when Kenny returned, he dangled a news clipping that questioned why someone would want to destroy such a thing.

I became wary. Again (for having lost my bearing, I am overconscious of you), wary seems understated. But that was it: wary. For I pretended, as did Kenny, that things had to die before they could be released into a better form. Slow, reasonable change was a lie.

There were other complications, too, by the time Bobby had been caught on the night we stole the tree. The main one was Dara. I had met her when she was still entranced by Kenny; I had dreamed of her and loved her image secretly since long before. She was, as I saw it—with her long, straight blond hair, her scarf and sports car—Kenny's contradiction. Or was Kenny hers? I knew she disliked Kenny's popping up at her apartment, wind-blown and tired. And yet he apparently was necessary for her, like a boat for the empty dock. Perhaps, though, that is another story. It is hard to tell.

Anyway, Kenny had left the day after we got the tree and by the time he breezed back into the house looking much like a sailor who's just come through a squall, there sat Bobby in all his commonness.

"Damn it. Damn it to hell." Kenny began to pace the breadth of the living room, across to the tree and back toward the Cuban flag hung on the wall.

"Stop that!" he ordered Bobby, who was still toying with the gauze wrapped around his thigh. Before Kenny had returned, Bobby had been showing me with ingenuous pleasure the neat tear one of the barbs had made in his thigh. He was fascinated by the way the muscle split wider, as if compelled to expose the bone.

Bobby pouted. Kenny stopped his pacing to wave his hand, pushing his anger aside for a moment, grinning apologetically at him. Kenny seemed actually to care for Bobby.

"Somebody sold us out," Kenny said, glaring at me. His eyes, red in the whites, were intense. He suspected me. And yet he was as happy as Beast, who lolled her head on Bobby's good leg. I tried to avoid Kenny's eyes by staring past him at the pictures tacked on the wall beside the tree. One was of Mao swimming the Yellow River—the one in which only Mao's head showed above the water's surface. Another was of a woman, a peasant, with a scythe. I wondered why the Chinese had done such a poor job, cutting Mao's head from another photograph and pasting it against a picture of the Yellow River. The fake was so stylized.

Bobby looked at me knowingly as Kenny stamped out of the room. I doubt that Bobby would have wanted us to dynamite the jail, especially not over a Christmas tree and a small fine. But I was unsure how truly knowing Bobby was, and so did not dare speak this to him. "Dara?" I said. Bobby shrugged as best he could beneath the weight of Beast. I took this to mean that he was willing to accept the possibility that Dara had paid his fine and gotten him released. We waited.

"Somebody's gotta pay for this," Kenny hissed slowly, as he returned, buttoning up the cuff of his sleeve—and he was gone.

Oh, Lord, I wonder, why didn't I see? Had I looked closely, I might have realized that the Chinese Junk which floated on the Yellow River was not seaworthy, that it, like the head that swam without arms or legs, was mocking my willingness to overlook things. And Dara: I never knew how much Kenny knew of what was happening between Dara and me. I have always thought that brothers should have been able to talk about such things. But the occasion never presented itself. Or, if it did, it was at inopportune times, as when we were on Kenny's motorcycle and I was busy jiggling the carburetor cable to keep us from overrunning a car in front of us. Besides, I was not sure how to begin. And I didn't know myself what was happening until it was too late.

Funny. There are things in life which are not only left unfinished but never, when we look back, seem to have begun. Rarely does the lack of completion matter, but in this case it seems to. At least it mattered to Kenny. For me, the incomplete hangs like a vast impenetrable fog over the placid gulf of my memory, and the redolence of this story can be contained, like Beast, only by what Kenny called a storm watch.

I SEE NOW HOW ODD WERE THE THINGS WHICH BEGAN TO HAPPEN. AT times, Kenny would move about the house planning, talking coherently, rapidly. Then, just as unexpectedly, he would be standing in the doorway, braced against the frame, sounding like a long-playing record slowed to 16 rpms. At those times Bobby and Beast would sit up all night trying to keep Kenny conscious, Bobby's fingers on Kenny's wrist, searching.

Or I'd return from the market, silently lamenting the cost of filet mignon, which I pulled from the large pockets of my overcoat (I was supposed to be stealing them), and trying to smile. Dark, indistinguishable faces grouped around some contraband on the floor would greet me. Even the laughter of those people frightened me and so, with faked bravado, I said hello and slipped off to my room where I hid with a book.

Sometimes Dara would tap lightly on my door and we'd talk. At first, she wanted to explain to me how she felt about Kenny. I didn't want to hear (why is it that brothers are expected to listen to such things?). She worried, too, about the strange people Kenny was bringing into the movement and into the house—their voices seemed to carry a threat like a red morning sky, and Dara began to long for silence. Eventually, our talk turned toward ourselves.

"Why," Dara wondered, "do we have to become a part of it in fighting it?"

It was a question we never answered, Dara and I, although we sensed that the storm which gathered around us was dissipating, losing its center—which for both of us had once been Kenny.

We were losing heart. Sure, not a little of our own vanity was involved. After all, we had been in contact with a movement's pulse for over a year, and each of us liked to believe that he was an important part of the world of action, of change—of history itself. But the center, captained by Kenny, was moving away from us—or we from it. We turned to each other for protection against the realities.

Kenny seemed to be cut adrift, and somehow his drifting was related to the tree. As I look back through the time between—that set of broken mirrors—all I see is Kenny, lopping branches from the tree with his Mexican switchblade.

Actually, I saw Kenny chop a branch from the tree only once that I remember, on Christmas Eve. By then the tree had been thinned quite a bit and was pitiful in the way it balanced on its three-footed stand, hinting at its original fullness. It was a sorry sight.

Christmas Eve, the night Kenny tried to stab me.

Dara and I had gotten up and had just put the angel on the top of the tree. My fingertips still tingled with the pleasure of holding her lightly as she stretched to set the angel in place. "Does it bother you," she said, "what is happening to Kenny? Do you ever feel it's our fault?"

"What?" I said.

"Well, you know. . . ."

"Don't you worry about it," I said. "We'll survive. We'll go on."

"You bastards," Kenny said. I hadn't heard him come in. But there he stood, looking at the two of us with eyes that shifted in his thinning face.

"Put the knife down, Kenny," I said.

I guess I should have left it at that. "You won't," I told him, instead. "You know you won't."

"Won't?" he muttered.

He seemed to lunge forward, almost tripping, and I knocked the knife aside and swung my left hand hard into his head behind the ear. He fell like an anchor. Dara moaned and knelt beside him, but he shoved her back on her rear and looked up at me. "So this is what it comes to," I thought, "the captain and the mate." It seemed as if seven different expressions flickered over his face as he looked at me. He stood, and we faced each other forever before he walked out of the house muttering. Dara called after him, and started to go. I grabbed her wrist and held it. She seemed to pull against me like a dock in a swell which creaks against the lines and then falls back. "Don't," I said. "Let him go. He'll be back."

I was right, too. Bobby brought him back in the middle of the night. "Help me get him upstairs," Bobby said, shaking me as though I were asleep. "He's in the van."

"My God," I said when I saw him. "What happened?"

"The bull." Bobby breathed hard as we dragged Kenny up the stairs. It wasn't easy. His body felt as though it were packed with water.

"Watch his head," I said. "Where?"

"Shipyard."

Why Kenny had tangled with a bull at the docks, I couldn't imagine. Those guards were not only tough and mean—they were afraid. Kenny's hands were cut badly, and bruised, and his skin felt clammy. And from a purple spot on his head on the side where I'd hit him was a dried trickle of blood which outlined the hollow of his cheek in the moonlight.

Dara and Bobby tried to wake Kenny up, to bring him back to life.

Bobby wouldn't let me call a doctor. Dara refused to look at me and, as the task grew more difficult, another feeling began to supplant my astonishment and sadness. Resentment grew slowly, became disgust, and finally rage. The silence was unbearable. We were stupefied sailors, becalmed on the China Sea. I went out to walk in the moonlight, to listen, to think.

MAYBE I WAS WRONG. THAT IDEA HAS JUST POPPED INTO MY HEAD AS I sit here in the warm shaft of light on the deck, writing. For in a sense, Kenny never returned. Although Bobby brought him home that night, he never regained consciousness. But what does that mean?

After the inquest, which was complicated to say the least, we packed up our things, sold the house, and began to explore, going from place to place. Dara and I, that is. After a bout with hepatitis, Bobby joined one of those mystical orders in California—and now he sits around most of the day, chanting. I guess that's not much different from what I do. Anyway, on the twenty-first of March we sailed for St. Thomas, and there took berths on a Greek ship bound for the Mediterranean. I worried that the Greek sailors might be a problem with Dara (in spite of her illness, she is still beautiful, though more ethereal), but they are behaving like a troop of Boy Scouts, trying to help her learn the Greek alphabet.

It seems we have bypassed the typhoon, and so I am left to myself, for the most part, on deck. I used to like to be alone. But on this ship it is as if the silence has become a scream in nature which lifts before the bow and passes overhead, converging with the mist of the wake behind. I wish I knew Greek. Then I could converse with the helmsman, at least.

Sometimes I think Dara holds against me my not attending the funeral, but I'm not sure. There were too many things to be arranged. Only at times do I wonder if there were not other reasons, reasons I ignored as I carefully put away the few monochrome ornaments and the string of lights. I will ask Dara, someday, when her health is better. She has suffered greatly these last months (does she blame herself?), and so it is we go where we go.

Yesterday, she almost laughed when I reminded her of some silly thing Beast once did. And with time, she may come to laugh often again, if I can teach her to expect things not to change. Until I can, I fear there will be no pleasure in being held by her. Probably it is why I have this impulse to pray.

I have given up the hope for change. Sure, you can do little things within the limits. But the kind of change we worked for, fought even each other for, seems, now, absurd. We seem to live in a morning fog, unable to see beyond the rails. Perhaps I am wrong: You decide. For I have sailed around it, Kenny through it, and his cargo of anger and love has been dumped, like Beast's drooling head, in my lap.

I do not, even yet, know quite what to do with it except beg.

But for what? for what?

I write to find out, to discover if things could have been different, but this is the conclusion I always come to.

In Dreams Begins Reality

MY FIRST WIFE WAS MAD. OR SO MY SISTER SAID. "SHE WAS CRAZY AS A loon, Albert," she'd say. She never said it while we were happily married, but waited until things had fallen apart. I think of the times we visited my sister and I came out of the shower in the morning to find my wife hunched on the edge of the makeshift bed in her hot-pink flannels, eating her breakfast with the door closed, and I wish my sister had said something earlier. But when I remember the look on my wife's face as she explained why she was eating in the bedroom instead of with my sister and her husband, I am unconvinced. She didn't sound like a madwoman.

"They either sit there reading and ignoring me," she said, "or she berates him for keeping her awake all night with his snoring. It makes me uncomfortable."

"That's just the way she is," I'd say.

The second wife, my sister said, was dull as brass. "She's a very nice person, Albert. But what do you have in common?"

Again she waited until I was alone, nightly trying to find a way to make the king-sized bed seem less like the Wallowa Valley. It was comforting to know I hadn't made a mistake. That's what sisters were for, I figured, like codeine. And I was grateful.

My sister never met the hat-trick wife. She was a hinter. You know the type, the woman who warns you a hundred times a day in small unnoticeable ways that something is wrong. She hints so much that your only recourse is to mistake her meaning. When she came home and said, What did I want for dinner, pork? Or just the fat? I pretended she was being humorous.

When she asked the same question about lamb—"You want some lamb? Or you just want me to slice off the fat and heat it up in the micro?"—I took her seriously and weighed my choices.

"Lamb would be fine," I said. "Thank you very much. Dear." She was dressed in a gregarious sheath of red. "Nice dress," I said.

"I'm going out later," she replied.

Sometimes, I'd try to participate in the hinting, make it fun. Like when we went to her sister's to look at wedding pictures and generally gush and glow over her sister's actually getting married. There was a picture of the rear of me, my feet and head lopped off by the viewfinder.

"Is it the same on a tug? Is port left and starboard right?" the wife asked her sister as they looked at the picture. Her sister squirmed. So as not to embarrass her, I joined in.

"That's not a tugboat," I said, grinning.

The wife gave me a piercing look.

"More like Moby-Dick with a tie."

The wife didn't laugh.

"Put cameras and 'Goodyear' on it and run it up in the air and it'll shoot the Super Bowl," I said.

The wife shot me a look that felt like the searing flames of hatred.

We divorced. "Three's the charm," I said, and decided that I was through with women. A hat trick's enough by anyone's measure. I have made an effort to remain friends with her, mostly for the sake of our love's by-product, Alicia, who is six.

She's still a hinter. Talking with her on the phone just now, I was regaling her with my theory that the president we see giving a prepared speech is really the brilliant artistry of an automatist, the careful modulations of the recorded voice the secret of Dolby. "That's why the real man seems so stupid at press conferences. It's not just that he is virtually incapable of a solitary logical thought. It's the contrast between art and life that really brings it home."

"Still as much fun as always," the ex-wife hinted.

"That a question or a statement?" I asked. "How's my little girl, anyway?"

"She's right here. Want to speak to her? Alicia," I could hear the ex-wife say, "come listen to your father. Yes, *now*."

"Hello, Father," Alicia said.

"Hi, precious. How's my little pumpkin?"

"Father!" Alicia complained. She doesn't like these affectionate nicknames. Thinks she's outgrown them. I try not to use them, but I can't help myself. As with a full half of what I say, the words just slip out when I'm not looking.

"When are you going to come up for a visit?" I asked.

"Don't know. It's so far."

"Maybe that's true, honeybunch. But I'd be happy to come down and get you, if your mother is afraid of the subway." Alicia lives with her mother in the East Village. I live at the far reaches of the Upper West Side. "Or I'll send you cab fare."

"Maybe after the Bahamas. Richard's taking Mommy and me to the Bahamas next month."

"I know," I said.

"Richard bought me a new bathing suit just for the trip. It's red. He's gonna teach me to scuba-dive."

"That Richard sounds like quite a guy. By the way, do you know what the letters in 'scuba' stand for?"

"Do I have to?" Alicia sighed.

"No. No, Richard will probably tell you anyway. 'Self-contained underwater breathing apparatus' people are like that. They like you to know the rituals and symbols of their sport. They're like sailors. Like dieters or people into meditation. . . ."

"Father," Alicia interrupted. "What's a wonk?"

"Why, sweetcakes? Where'd you hear that word?"

"Richard."

"Yeah?" I wasn't sure I liked Richard teaching my babydoll such language. Where did it lead?

"Yeah. He says you're a real—"

"So, Albert," the ex-wife's voice said after a scuffle over the receiver. "We've got to run along. The Bottom Line is playing Trump's Trumps this afternoon."

"What in the world is 'the bottom line'?"

"Richard's softball team," the ex-wife said. "Talk to you later. Maybe you should get out and join a softball team. Be good for you. And you could supply the team with chatter."

I can take a hint. "If I do, will you come back to me? Would you love me again?"

"I'll make Alicia send you a postcard from the Bahamas," she said. She hung up.

NORMALLY I KEEP SUNDAYS TO MYSELF, RESERVING TIME TO BROWSE through the *Times* and time to think up letters to the editor of the book review section. These letters range from chilling attacks on the entire section to letters with specific focus. I never send these letters, at least in part because I never write them. I think them. Taking the time to write them would waste precious Sunday minutes.

After shaming the book review editor, I stroll down to Zabar's and buy fresh bagels, then cut over to Columbus and stop by the deli to pick up chopped Nova lox, then home again to eat them both with cream cheese, while I decide what to do with the rest of the day. Most Sundays, this deciding takes me into late afternoon, at which point I allow myself to look through the television section and start thinking about having a drink before dinner. With mixed emotions, I decide this Sunday to get out and get some exercise. By the boat pond in the park, radio-controlled sailboats compete for attention with radio-controlled roller skaters. In a vee of grass among the trees, the pitched laughter of twelve Asians playing volleyball sounds like the delicate and oddly beautiful plink of Eastern music. A girl on the frontier of womanhood and leaning to tart buys ice cream from a vendor's cart, her red nylon stretch pants drawing L's—from lust and longing to leers and leaving. Her pants are so revealing that she almost achieves the nun-like innocence of the overclothed. The feeling of her as I walk away stays with me like the sunrise over Makrialos.

I sit on a bench and watch sides being chosen for a pickup softball game, imaginatively penning another letter to the *Times*. A woman comes over and asks me if I want to play. Her name is Gail. Even with her dirty blond hair held back by a headband you can tell Gail has what can only be called big hair.

"No. Thank you."

"We can use another player," she says.

"You've got a backstop," I say. She just looks perplexed. "Well, what the heck. Okay." I figured I'd play catcher.

Gail borrows a glove for me from the other team and assigns me third base, a position I want about as much as another divorce. I'm no better at third base than I am at marriage or poker, preferring low-risk bets like catcher to the high stakes of double plays and charging grounders.

Gail takes shortstop. In all my years of watching softball, this hasn't happened often, but Gail looks as though she can handle the job. Indeed, Gail seems eager, ready, willing, and able to field grounders, pop-ups, and line drives, as well as to egg on those of us less eager or able. As the first baseman lobs grounders at us and warms us up she moves with grace and not a little strength. Her chatter as the game begins sounds like any shortstop's chatter. Except for the pitch of her voice and the fact that despite her big hair Gail is pretty, she could be Phil Rizzuto. Pee Wee Reese. The girl in red comes over and stands there, tongue licking about the rim of her ice cream cone, watching. She suddenly takes me back to days when little boys played softball and little girls looked appealingly on from the sidelines, careful not to show too much calf between their bobby socks and the hems of their full skirts.

Days of an uneasy détente when our mothers apprenticed us to the world of action by telling us to stop moping around the house and go out and kill off a tribe or two of Indians. (Moping was for girls and when Mother's friends heard that I liked books more than ball, they coughed.) Days of a recurring boyhood dream: I'm at third base, a huge white softball bouncing ten feet in front of me and beginning to spin. With the instinct of Brooks Robinson, I understood that the second bounce would send the ball kicking over my head, so I charged it and knocked it down heroically. Feeling the little girls smile from the sidelines, I concentrated on keeping my wits about me. I picked up the ball and looked toward first. "I'm making a play," I thought, and realizing that I was making a play, I threw the ball hard at the first baseman.

The ball orbited over first base, returned to earth a good forty feet beyond, and rolled white and solitary for a decade. Long enough for the shortstop to stroll over and force himself to say, "It's all right. We'll get the next batter." Long enough for the sidelined girls to giggle and twitter and point, and for me to hate their twittering. I'd awaken, swearing off softball, swearing that I would show those girls, that I'd never let this happen again.

But it did. It happened again, again and again, over thirty-odd years. Crouching there beside Gail, I see how I'm a sucker for games. How if there was one to be played, I played it.

I come to life like the stone guest in *Don Giovanni* as a hard-hit grounder—mine—skips to my left. Gail slides deep into the hole behind me, knocks the ball down, and, despite the thrill of making the play, decides against throwing to first. The men on the opposing team's bench smile secretly. Chagrined, I look away and see the girl in nylon red pants poke the last of her ice cream cone through her lips and smirk.

"Sorry," I mutter to Gail. "Daydreaming."

"S'okay," Gail says. "We'll get the next batter." She smiles and slaps me on the rear end, coach-like, and for a moment I feel, deep down, an awakening of the simple innocence of my boyish heart. I believe we will get the next batter, Gail and I, if only I can pay attention. I crouch, eye on the next batter and ready for the pitch, determined not to let Gail down, marveling at the way things change. Had little girls giggled and twittered not at me but because they were denied the chance to make the same errors? I was grateful for the way some of them had grown up, giving up limp-wristed dainty flings, learning to throw from the shoulder.

I was grateful for Gail and I was amused by the antics of the men on the other team, celebrating their victory with lots of expensive-looking beer. "If only I'd caught that pop-up," I said.

"What the hell," Gail said. "It's only a game. See you next week?"

"Maybe," I said.

"Maybe we'll try you at catcher."

"Sure. Whatever. Even backstop." Gail didn't get it and I let it go. We said goodbye.

Heading past the boat pond out of the park, the roller skaters had been replaced by a bunch of boys bouncing like popcorn to the dulcet strains of their rap music on a ghetto blaster. "Ghetto-blasting their way right out of the power structure," I think. "Right out of time." I think about the girl in red pants. She, too, seems out of time, like an illusion from the past which has become a present anachronism. Maybe she would grow up like Gail. Then again, maybe she wouldn't.

"Anything's possible," I think, and then I say it, out loud, making a pretzel vendor wonder if I am speaking to him or, like so many in this city, simply speaking to anyone who might be listening. For the first time in years, I know what to do with the rest of my Sunday. Go downtown and buy Alicia a softball glove. Maybe some sweatpants. Some loose blue sweatpants.

Grab Hold

JACOB FELT THE FAINT STIRRING OF A FEELING HE USED TO ASSOCIATE with the compression of the lungs around the smoke of a cigarette on a muggy summer's night. It was a precipitous feeling of emptiness, a hunger not in the stomach but in the cavity above the fundus.

Jane and he had just finished making love. "Sliding love," he liked to call it because of the sweat and humidity which made him feel the whole time that he was falling off the edge of the bed. He lay back panting, elbows jutting up at a right angle to each other, hands clasped beneath his head on the pillow, complaining of the heat.

"Lord, what I wouldn't give for a little breeze," he said.

The flat air felt as if it were pressing down upon him, pinning him to the pillow. Not flat, actually, but nearly solid: as though between his physical body and the wall, between the wall and the one dying tree in the yard, there was not air but some liquid substance, like mercury. And there was not only no breeze but, if possible, the absolute opposite of breeze.

"Umm," Jane said. She pawed about on the floor for her cigarettes. She had to switch on the shadeless lamp near the bed and he admired her back. Jacob liked women's backs. Given, for example, a choice among photographs of naked women, he would choose the one of a woman half-clothed, with only her back revealed. He thought he could see the greatest amount of character, if any, in backs, and it was women's backs he had seen the most of. Jane extracted two cigarettes, handed one to him, and they lit up in silence, lying there staring at the stucco ceiling.

"Anything wrong?" he asked. Even though they only dated off and on now, they had lived together before and he understood that her silence meant she was holding something back from him.

"Huh? No," she said, crushing her cigarette and handing the ashtray to him before switching off the light. She sighed with the heat as he unstuck himself from the sheets and padded for the refrigerator. He came back.

"Don't you have any beer?"

"None in the fridge?"

"No." He was irritated.

"Look in the cupboard." Her voice was sleepy.

"Warm beer?"

"Guess I forgot. . . ." She yawned and turned over in the bed.

"Christ!" he muttered as he went back to the kitchen. Popping a tab from a can, he drew a large gulp, set the other five in the freezer, and went into the living room and flicked on the TV. "Christ," he said to the emcee who was hyping the same brand of beer, "she forgot."

She was asleep when he returned to bed and the moonlight filtered in through the cheap white curtains like light at the bottom of a lake. She had pulled the top sheet over herself and he looked at the lumps of her figure. The sheets were white with blue shoots of bamboo criss-crossing them in large squares like a net. He shoved the collie-sized poodle aside with his foot and crawled up next to the stone wall of the room.

This was his low period and he needed comfort, love, affection; some-one's arms around him in the night. But it was too hot.

THE NEXT MORNING THEY MADE LOVE AGAIN AND STILL SHE HELD BACK from him, as though she wished he were someone else. His mind wobbled. Was there someone else? He rejected the possibility. Jane got up to take a shower.

"Hey," he said, "let's take one together." She had liked to do this even though he was clumsy at it. Locked into a little stall with her, he had always had to concentrate on not doing damage to her person, rather than on the sensuality of the experience. Usually he had turned down her requests but today he was trying to bring her back toward him, to open her up.

She looked back at him from the hall and finally said, "Okay, come on," in a voice that did not relieve his worry at all. In the tiled bathroom, she reached into the stall and turned the hot water full on.

"My God," he said, "that's going to take off our skin."

"I've got to have it high," she said, adjusting the "cold" knob, "to get all of the shampoo out of my hair." A small chunk of grout fell loose from between the tiles that the stream sprayed on, swirled around the floor of the stall, and in a single rush, swept into the drain. He was about to follow her in when he slipped and slapped back on the floor, his head just missing the rim of the toilet. His eyes riveted to the fright which made her eyes glassy. "Jacob! My God. Are you all right?" She knelt beside him, cradling his head in her arms.

"Watch that first step," he said, grinning. He was pleased at her reaction and he allowed himself to listen to the echo of her sobbing exclamation before getting up.

"For God's sake, be careful," she said, her previous tone seeping through her concern like water through a badly caulked seam.

Jacob stayed in the shower for a long time after she had toweled herself dry and considered his situation: Did his coming back to her, did her abortion, make a difference? He heard the phone ring and Jane answer. He could not hear what she said or guess who it was on the other end of the line. She talked for several minutes and, as he turned off the water, he heard her hang up. He felt suddenly afraid.

"Who was that?" he asked, as he emerged from the steaming bathroom, attempting to make his voice sound disinterested and jovial.

"When?"

"Just now. On the phone."

"Just a friend." She sat before a reconditioned vanity desk and in the mirror he saw her glance quickly up and then away. It seemed to him that her eyes carried either fear or warning, but he wasn't sure which.

"Umm," he uttered. He tried to let it pass. He knew better than to force her to tell him what he did not want to hear. When they'd split up, Jacob had demanded that she not tell him anything about other men. It was better, he thought, for him, if he didn't know. And she'd agreed, although she relented when he made the mistake of pressing her for details.

"How 'bout tonight?" he asked her.

"I can't."

"Why not?"

"I'm busy."

"With what?" Her silence told him all he needed to know and he meant to leave it at that. Let it go, he told himself, it's a can of worms.

"Come on," he said. "You can tell me." And for a moment he believed she really could. She had on a thin cotton blouse which buttoned in the back. He could see the line of her bra and down at the waist a portion of her back where the blouse parted. He stood behind her and traced with his finger the curve of her spine above her pants. God, that back, he thought. "Come on, Jane," he said softly.

"Jacob! Jesus, *you're* the one who doesn't want to hear. Remember?"

He remained silent.

She turned. "You still don't believe the baby was yours. Do you?"

"Okay," he said. "It doesn't matter."

"Look. You make up your mind how you want it and you can have it that way." She seemed to be holding back a scream. "But for God's sake, make up your little mind."

"Okay, okay," he said, clenching his fists. "Okay."

"SOME CLOWN FROM WORK?" HE SAID. THEY LOUNGED BENEATH THE skeletal shade tree in front of Jane's house. "Bet he wears a double-knit. Got a fancy car." He smiled, trying to make his sarcasm piercing, but sensed that he had failed and had merely sounded grim.

"The devil has green wings," she said. "This guy isn't a clown."

"The devil doesn't," he said, unwilling to let her say things unchallenged. "And I bet this guy is."

"The devil's wings are green," she said. She left her date for the approaching evening (or worse, he thought, night) out of it. The evenness of her voice took Jacob up and held him as though he were on a diaphanous plane which threatened to tear suddenly and let him—make him—fall beneath the surface, through miles of layered cotton batting.

"How do you know?" He closed his eyes. He regretted having introduced the habit of conversation in which apparent nonsense was used to say something important. He was tired of riddles. His entire life had become a riddle. "How do *you* know?" he said.

"I've seen him. When he's jealous." She hissed, her tongue a flutelike instrument held against the roof of her mouth. He moved behind her and snared her in the vee of his legs, kissing her neck beneath the wisps of hair which had slipped loose from the barrette, holding his breath to keep the hair from tickling his nostrils and making his nose twitch, or worse, sneeze. He felt the warm moisture of the grass against his jeans and wondered if there would ever be an end to this sweating.

"Don't," Jane said. His hand had crept toward her breast.

"Why not?" he said. Living with her, he had failed to believe in open relationships and free expression. He had not been able to forget what his parents had taught him. But there on the sweating grass, he wanted to try again.

Jane rolled out of the vee onto her belly and stared across the street, down a cul-de-sac where a fat girl in a shabby pink dress threw stones across the street at a little black boy.

Jacob remembered the idyll of his own childhood in a neighborhood much like this one. The woman down the street—the milkman brought her milk in a brown paper bag and stayed half an hour in his delivery. And Shepherd Lady across the street, the moral custodian of the block who walked with heavy stealth to parental doors to turn the children in when they swore. For such things, he had been severely punished. The suppliers of sex and morality are all gone, Jacob thought, having accomplished nothing, nothing at all.

"You're not listening," Jane said.

"Yes I am." A battered camper-laden pickup truck rounded the corner, swaying. Jacob saw the mouth of a curlered head in the passenger window form two syllables aimed at him as the muffler roared. He rolled over, straddling Jane on the lawn. "Let's . . . ," he said. But she toppled him off.

"Oh Jane," he said. "Oh, Jane." He wanted to be sorry for everything. He wanted to make promises of all kinds and magnitudes but all he could say was, Oh, Jane.

"It's time you better go," she said. "I've got to rest."

Low period. Jacob wondered how low he could get before some small act would begin his upswing. It had gone on for a year. Ever since, in fact, he had run out on Jane, moved out of the house they had shared with five other people. Things were not helping him any, lately.

God, it was hot. The heat made it impossible to think clearly, to see things as they were. There were always the minute crystals of salt beading on his eyelashes, refracting the light into strands of separate color.

He wished he had his van and didn't have to walk, but he had smashed the van up the month before, glancing off a power pole and flipping over a low dike into the rice fields bordering the road. He stopped at an In-and-Out market and bought a quart of beer, which he gulped on his way home.

He could see a letter inside his mailbox at the apartment. Having lost the key long ago, he pried the tin box open to find a third and final notice that the electric company was shutting off his electricity if he did not pay his bill immediately. Oh well, he thought. It was easy enough to turn the power back on—cut the lead seal and flip the switch on the meter. Still, it enraged him that the company threatened in this way, without taking into account how hard times were. He held the notice up in front of him and glared at Reddy Kilowatt's face, which, like Kilroy's, was frowning and red. "You'll be sorry, Reddy, my friend," he muttered, "if you keep this up." Last time he'd had a bout with the power company, he'd taken a hammer to the rows of electric meters, for which he'd spent some time in jail.

His air conditioner was off. He looked at the due date on the bill. They were prompt, no doubt about that. He opened the refrigerator and felt the milk. It was still cool but by no means cold. In the freezer, the ice cubes swam in individual pools of water. Draining the water off, he used the remaining slivers of ice to make himself a drink, and lay down on the couch and tried to think.

Through the plywood walls he could hear Morris, the self-taught blues singer, practicing. Upstairs, the charismatic Christian was doing push-ups again, and the regular squeaking of the floor above Jacob's head made him think of Jane. He tried to think of something else, but he couldn't. He pulled the phone over and was relieved to hear the dial tone, which he listened to for a few minutes before he replaced the receiver. He had to do something, go somewhere, get moving.

"USUAL?" ROBIN, THE BARMAID, STROLLED OVER TO WHERE HE SAT alone near the TV set. A baseball game was on and he abstractedly watched grown boys trotting about, playing at their million-dollar game. The bar was sparsely populated. It was still early.

"I'll stick to beer," he said. He had not eaten and he believed that he had better stay light.

"Draft?"

"Dos Equis." Robin drifted off toward the glass-doored cooler. In the mirror behind the bar he could see a young woman let a man in a quiet suit run his fingers up and down the blond hair on her arm. "And a couple of those embryos," he said, as Robin set the bottle before him. He nodded toward a glass jar filled with brownish liquid in which pickled eggs crowded together trying to float.

"Nothing on tonight?" she asked.

"Nah. Not yet." He winked at her as though to say the night wasn't over.

"Say. You read about the poles of the earth flipping over?" His face must have expressed his confusion. Robin bent down and pulled out a *National Enquirer.* "It says here," she went on, thumbing to the page, "that the polar ice cap is expanding. If it keeps going like it is, getting bigger, it might make the axis of the earth rotate and put the North Pole where the South Pole is now. It'd make the earth crack. People are worried about it."

Jacob had not caught the contagion of fear. In fact, he had not noticed that people were worried about it. "I suppose they'll do something to prevent it," he said. He finished his beer. "Listen. Give me a six-pack to go, okay?" He tossed three dollars on the bar.

"Equis?"

"Anything with a twist top," he said.

The man in the suit said something to the young woman and jerked his head toward the door. She shook her head, no, smiling as if to extract a promise from him not to get angry but buy her another drink, instead.

Other people have problems, Jacob thought, watching the man force his face into passivity. It was a lottery. The man buys her drinks, hoping that his number will come up and she'll go home with him. Without destroying his hopefulness, she keeps the numbers tumbling, allowing some of the right numbers to come up but never in the right sequence. Everyone knew it was a game and yet everyone played it repeatedly with the same forbidding odds. Jacob's vision blurred. For an instant the woman looked like Jane, was Jane to him. He was grateful that she was saying no to the man.

"Something wrong?" Robin returned with his beer and his change.

"No." She was watching his face. "See you," he said, slipping off his stool. On his way out he bumped the man's elbow, causing his drink to splash onto the bar. "Give up," he whispered. He kept on walking even when the man said, "Watch it, punk." Punk? Jacob thought. Maybe I ought to. . . . But he decided that it was too easy. The odds were not heavy enough.

He found himself walking along the railroad tracks behind the warehouses bordering Third Street. Nobody walked that section of town, not alone, not at night. Jacob hummed to himself as though the gravelly sounds he heard behind him were only the echo of his own footsteps. He figured there were at least three of them following him, but they were laying back, watching him. He stopped and peed on a stack of lumber, spelling out "J-a-n-e."

As he opened his last bottle of beer and tossed the cap onto the tracks, a figure stepped out from behind another stack of lumber and straight-armed him in the chest, and Jacob reeled backward into the grasp of two other boys. The first figure began to move in on him and he could see the fists hanging on the ends of the boy's half-lifted arms. Suddenly, he realized that this was what he wanted, action, something to occur which demanded a winner, a loser.

Joy spread through him as though he were transparent and the feeling was light, and the next thing Jacob knew, the first figure was doubled on the ground clutching his groin and Jacob was running, winded by laughter. The two other boys were vanishing in the darkness which spread out before him like heaven. Jacob ran down the tracks behind them, the adrenaline and the wet air in his lungs scraping the edge of his nerves clean of twelve months. So this was what it took. One figure swerved from the path, clung momentarily to a high chain-link fence, and then scrambled over it as Jacob ran past him. The other figure dodged into the ink black of an alley. Still Jacob ran, the tracks like a ladder, gently sloping down—down, he knew then, to Jane's house, to the one place he should not go.

He pounded on her door, causing lights to be switched on in a path from the bedroom to the front door. Jane opened it and he cried, "You were right!" before she could say anything. She could see that he wept. But could she see that this time it was not from sadness, not from fear, but out of joy?

"Jacob!" She was angry. Yet there was a flaw in the tone of her anger.

"Get rid of him!" Jacob cried. "Send him home. Come to my house." He was out of breath and panting. "Get rid of him. You were right. But the ice . . . the ice, Jane." He began flapping his arms as though he would fly and started down her driveway, away from the house. He stopped at the end of the driveway and turned. She still stood there, backlit by the illumination from inside. "Please," he whispered. "Please."

AT HOME HE SLEPT. IN HIS DREAM HE SAW A FIGURE WITH GREEN WINGS pushing at the axis of an immense blue sphere and the degrees clicking off on a digital counter: 23, 28, 35. . . . When he awoke, he began to work his way methodically through his apartment, upturning the sofa and chairs and removing the tags that said, "Do not remove. . . ." Then he stripped the sheets from the bed and neatly replaced the coverlet and went into the kitchen and took out a grocery sack with the question "What Price Have You Been Paying?" printed on it in red. He began to fill the sack with cans and bottles, half empty or full, which he carried out to the large green Dumpster behind the apartment building. He left the door unlocked when he came back in.

He showered and dressed in clean night clothes, and lay down on the coverlet. His left arm rested on his hip, and his knees pulled up slightly in the shape of an anchor. As he crossed the threshold into sleep, he thought he could hear the ice shift. He felt the earth move, and he grabbed hold. He believed she would come. He had to believe that.

Star Lake, Long Ago

WE WERE SITTING OVER OMELETS IN STAR LAKE, NEW YORK. IT WAS opening day on deer and we saw hunters lining the highway on our way into Ma's Friendly Hut; they were talking, hunching into orange and red coats, sipping coffee in steamy groups of bigness.

"What's wrong?" I said, wishing Angela would give me a break and try to tell me what she was pissed off about. I gave her an intent look, trying not to look weary or worn out. It was an endless story. This was closing day on the trip we'd taken to celebrate a new beginning, a departure from the troubles we'd been having. "Want to talk?"

"There's nothing to talk about."

There was an unlit neon sign in the front window. It said "Beer." I wanted to bang the table and make the cups rattle on their saucers, but the three women and boy to our left might not have appreciated a scene over their coffee and cigarettes.

"Here ya go, Lolly." The waitress set a plate in front of one of the women. The waitress was huge, and she panted from exertion after she spoke.

"Thank you," Lolly said, in that small-town, I've-lived-here-forever voice. She had a generous face, the kind of face that would be called pretty if it wasn't so packed with flesh. Her son's face had written all over it the confusion of growing up in Star Lake—farsighted, with those thick reversed lenses. He had what you'd call a stupid face, a slow face, neither kind nor mean but capable of either. You could tell that the most exciting day of his life wasn't Christmas or his birthday, but the opening of deer season. He'd been left behind today. You could see that he didn't like being left like that.

"Come on, Angela," I whispered.

She looked away.

"You want some more coffee?" I said, getting up and going across to the burners where the pots were kept warm. She shook her head like she was being slapped.

"Not yet," she said.

Oh, that voice! I knew that voice; I'd heard it plenty of times before, let me tell you. It was the kind of voice that uses one thing to say another, a low, threatening rasp like the sound of a crazy hunter edging through the brush.

"Yes now," our waitress said. "What'll it be for dessert?"

"Is it possible to have pie *and* cheese and ice cream?" Angela asked.

The waitress looked confused. "I don't see no reason why not."

"It's not on the menu," I explained.

"Oh, well. Ma'll fix you up anything you wants."

So there really was a "Ma," I thought. You expect that in places like Star Lake. "I'd like one, too," I said. "Apple and cheese. No ice cream." Angela gave me a look with her lips pinched together, as if she could cry. "What's the matter with that?" I said. She shrugged.

"You kids new here?" the waitress said.

"Just passing through," I said. "Sort of a honeymoon."

"That's nice. That's real nice," the waitress said. She looked at Angela. "Drinks?"

"With him, they happen real fast," Angela said.

I squirmed in my seat. "Just this coffee for me, thanks," I said.

"I'll have another large orange juice." Angela seemed to be laughing to herself.

"Can I change my mind? Sorry to be such a bother. I'll have orange juice, too, please."

"No bother." The waitress panted.

A man came in, dressed in a lined green windbreaker and jeans—baggy, loose jeans, the kind where if he knelt or bent over, his crack would show. "Hey, Dotty," he called. "Hube got his deer yet?"

"He will," Dotty, our waitress, answered. She smiled and her incisors were yellow and crooked. "Hube always does get his, don't he?"

"Wish he'd show some a us where he goes every year," the man said. He poured himself a Styrofoam cup of coffee, capped it, and, without paying, left, saying, "So long, now."

"After a while," a voice called from the kitchen. Ma, probably.

"My husband's the best hunter in these parts. Always gets something, the first day," Dotty explained. "Two pies and cheese, comin' right up."

She went into the kitchen, and through a window in the makeshift plywood wall dividing her from the friendly part of the hut, I saw her don an apron and begin slicing cheese.

"Wonder how he got her," I said to Angela.

Angela wasn't in the mood. She muttered something that sounded like "Wonder how I got you," but I wasn't sure. She looked up suddenly and said, "Can't you even make a decision about dessert on your own?"

"I changed my mind."

She was always irritated by what she called my lack of adventure, but I was tired and it seemed as though we'd been through it the day before—all the days before.

IF I'D RENTED A RUNABOUT, MAYBE ALL OF THIS WOULD NOT HAVE HAP-
pened. For all practical purposes, we were in love with each other,
Angela and I. Angela had wanted more than practical purposes, so we'd
taken a holiday, trying to escape from the day-to-day of our lives.

The proof had come when we'd set out from the shore by the cottage we'd rented, in a small boat with an 18-horse motor. It had snowed
the night before for the first time that year, and everything was white
and brown and cold along the docks, and Mr. Mallory, who rented us
the boat, warned us against the wind blowing up the lake. We were only
headed down to Windyridge Lodge for lunch—a trip he said wouldn't
take more than half an hour. It was meant to be a slight adventure.

Angela and I had been getting along swell up to the point of renting
that boat, although with Angela you can never tell. She'll smile and say
how happy she is, and let you relax, when all the time she has some small
bitterness cooking on a back burner. As soon as you let your guard down,
it'll all boil over. Still, she seemed to be relaxing, and I was managing just
fine; although I'm not one for adventure, I was faking it pretty well.

Mr. Mallory pull-started the engine for us, and revved it a few times.
Then we went into the shack to fill out the rental paperwork while the
engine warmed, smoking bluish against the dark green lake. "Sure you
don't want a runabout, instead?" he asked me. "Only three bucks an
hour more."

"No," I said. "Thanks."

"Suit yourself." His eyes had a peculiar gleam.

Mrs. Mallory showed me charts of the lake. It seemed to be a pretty
big lake, and I commented on that, only to hear husband and wife
agree—it was a pretty big lake. There were bays and inlets and delta-like
swamps. Red dots on the charts were marked in script, *many snags,
buried islands.*

"Stay away from here," Mrs. Mallory said. She pointed to a place
with three or four of those red dots. "Stay outta there. You'll catch trouble, you go in there."

She showed me how she and her husband went down to Windyridge. What I didn't think of was that she and her husband went on warm days and had had lots of practice running boats around the lake. The two of them were practiced; they could function as a team, no matter what the weather.

But I was confident. This was an adventure. Determined to display the heart of an explorer, I tossed the charts to Angela and said, "Take a look at those," while Mr. Mallory showed me how to slip the motor into forward and reverse. "Steer with your left hand," he told me.

"We've got to stay away from there," I said to Angela. "We should go this route." I drew a line with my thumbnail past Birch and Joe Indian Islands, across the edge of the lake to where Windyridge was supposed to be.

"Maybe we should rent a runabout," she said.

"Don't be ridiculous."

We set out. I cranked the 18 horses all the way up and the front of the boat lifted and bounced about as I got used to the steering.

"Sit down," I hollered over the noise of the motor. Angela was shifting from seat to seat, trying to stand upright instead of crawling and using all fours.

Birch Island wasn't much larger than an atoll, but we didn't know that. On the charts, it had size.

"Do you think that's it?" Angela asked.

"Couldn't be. No. Hell, there's no more'n three trees on that rock, and I don't think they're birch."

When we came to Joe Indian Island, it was Angela who figured that it had to be Birch Island, and I headed out into the open water, away from the buoys marking snags and shallows. Pretty soon, we were past it. The water had grown rough, the wind higher, and my left hand was getting cold while my jacket was beginning to soak through. Angela was a little better off, being farther up in the boat and lifted away from the spray which hit me every so often. We were cutting across wavelets; I zigged and zagged, trying to keep down the amount of spray. Finally, I throttled back.

"I knew it," I said.

We had gotten into *there*. The place Mrs. Mallory had said to stay away from, a delta system filled with snags hiding beneath the chopped surface of the shallow water or sticking up just above the water like the twisted claws of drowning people, beckoning.

I was scared. We were lost, and as I looked around, trying to find a familiar landmark, I could see the weather wasn't going to hold much longer.

I felt like when I was an adolescent and my mother had said, "Stay out of trouble," and I'd gone and gotten arrested. As I throttled the boat back again, I started shaking, wanting to cry because I felt so alone, but refusing to cry out of pride and hurt and hatred. With the wind coming up and the sky getting blacker, Angela may as well have been. . . . I was going to say dead, but that doesn't seem fair.

The boat began to drift and I grabbed at a snag, which broke off in my hand. I started yelling. Less at Angela at first than at my fright; then I began to blame her. Not for getting us lost—that wasn't her fault any more than it was my own—but for the way she was pulling back into herself, abandoning me to the delta of snags and my fear of dying from exposure after we capsized. I don't remember what it was I yelled; I do remember wondering why I was yelling at one of the people I cared for most in the world. I didn't have time to wonder much over that, though, since over the mountains the thunderheads were grouping like mailed fists about to pound us into oblivion.

"You could help, you know," I screamed. "Instead of sitting there like Cleopatra in her boat."

Angela just glared before she hung her head as if praying. She had this way of dropping her whole face down and then raising up her head, face, and those almond eyes in one smooth gesture, to reveal what she felt. I loved the way she did that, even though I knew that this time the way she felt was not nice. When she did speak, she accused me of staring at women in a theater we'd gone to once. How long that had been simmering in her mind, I had no idea.

I said gently, "I love you, Angela." It was, after all, true. I had since the night I followed her home from a party (she resented that, too—my following her home).

Either Angela ignored me or my words were lost in a burst of wind. We were heading, now, into the grin of the storm, and the way she sat cross-legged in the prow, pointing right or left and guiding us around snags or between small islets, she looked like Shiva with her several pairs of arms. I cursed her beneath the steam of my breath and changed hands on the throttle to keep from getting frostbite.

We never found Windyridge, but we did find our way back up the lake. By accident. When Angela threw the charts at my face, she'd missed me and the charts had sunk quickly in the heaving water before I could get a fix on them.

"Good," I said. "Now we'll have to replace those. That, of course, doesn't matter to you, does it? You're not paying for this honeymoon."

Soon enough, we'd begun to recognize landmarks along the shore, and sure of ourselves, we'd hurried in to the docks, pulling in just as the rain was turning to white, driving flakes of snow. Mr. Mallory had a runabout warming up on idle and Mrs. Mallory emerged from the engine house to greet us, wiping her hands in relief.

"We was beginning to worry," she said. "How was your lunch?"

Angela jumped out of the boat and strode past Mrs. Mallory up toward our cabin.

"It was fine," I said. I explained about the charts being blown overboard and gave her enough money to replace them. Then I wandered up the path after Angela.

She had her suitcase on the bed and was folding sweaters and jeans deliberately.

"What's this?" I said.

"I want to go home. I don't want to stay here."

I almost told her that I had the car keys, so she wasn't going anywhere, but I was so glad to be off the lake I said, "I'm sorry, Ange. I'm sorry for yelling. Really. I was scared."

She set a pair of pants into her case and straightened up, looking not at me but out the windows of the sleeping porch at the wet snow that swirled and stuck to the glass, melting down the panes. It was growing black outside and the lights of the Mallorys' house cast glints of yellow and white down by the docks.

"Angela." I touched her on the shoulder. Even beneath my baggy sweater that she was wearing, I could feel her flinch and soften and I smiled behind her back. "I love you."

That stopped her cold. It always did. She turned to me with an expression I didn't recognize. It could have been love. It could just as easily have been hate. I tried to pull her close so I wouldn't have to look at her glassy eyes and so she couldn't see the dregs of the smile which hadn't vanished quickly enough when she whirled toward me.

"My husband used to yell," she said, pushing away from me and sinking onto the bed, which sagged generously. "I can't take yelling. Sometimes we'd be driving along and he'd start screaming at me, pounding both fists on the dashboard while we were zooming down the highway. Not steering. Not paying attention. I was certain it was the end and we were going to be killed. . . ."

"You want some coffee?" I said.

I slipped into the kitchen and boiled water in the pot.

"I'm listening," I called. "Go on."

When I came back, I handed her the mug. "Careful, it's hot," I said.

She took the mug and slowly stirred sugar into it. The wind outside seemed to be dying back, the storm passing as swiftly as it had come up.

"He used to beat me up, sometimes."

The lights of the houses across the bay winked and went out as the clouds broke and then regathered, unwilling to give up the threat of snow and rain, and I felt calm at last.

"We can leave tomorrow, if you like. If it doesn't snow too hard tonight."

"Oh!" Angela said. "You haven't heard a word I've been saying." She threw her coffee at me and slammed out of the room and locked herself in one of the spare bedrooms we'd shut off to save on heat. I sat still and examined the coffee stains fixing themselves into my white sweater. I slipped it off and soaked it in cold water with a drop of dish detergent.

Standing by the door she had locked, I whispered, "Angela." No answer. I said louder that I was going out for a while, if she wanted to come along. Since there still wasn't any answer, I figured she needed some time alone—to think, to feel, to do whatever she did when she needed some time alone.

I walked the three miles to Cranberry Lake and listened to hunters in the local bar psyche themselves up for opening day. I feel uncomfortable around hunters, and after listening for some time I found myself fantasizing the deer carrying on similar conversations.

"Okay. Billy Buck, you head north."

"John Buck, you keep circling in a mile radius around the lake, and try to keep those assholes away from the fawns and does."

"Remember that one hunter with an eight-point belly?"

"Couldn't sneak up on a dead tree."

At that point, I knew it was time for me to be going. When I left to walk back, the sky was clear and you could hear the waves of the lake lapping at the pebbles along the shore and slapping dock pilings gently like a playful lover.

I GUESS I SHOULD HAVE HAD AN INTUITION OF THE END, THEN, IN THE dark of the night. And yet Angela and I had a lot going for us. Memories and such. I couldn't give up the belief that she would come back. It had to be a passing thing.

I'd crawled into bed alone, wrapping myself as best I could in the sole blanket Angela had not taken, and thinking about love. I was willing, then, to do almost anything to have her forgive me for raising my voice—and I was wishing that I had spent the extra money to rent a runabout.

When I awoke in the middle of my troubled sleep, she was there, mounting me, making love to me. I was half-dazed. It was like a dream: She had one hand on herself and the other around behind her thigh tickling me, her head thrown back and her voice making these wonderful whimpering sounds. When she came, it was like an electric fire was shocking through her veins and she shouted—words I'd never heard a woman shout before. I was sure the Mallorys could hear her down in their house, and I smiled at what they must be thinking.

After her orgasm, she kept moving, but I could feel in her rocking movements a growing sense of obligation or fairness. She was moving away from me. It was like watching a person withdrawing into an underground tunnel, going down the ladder one slow step at a time and pulling a trapdoor shut over her head. And when she slipped away to the other bedroom, the after-silence was as dark as the night sky after a single flash of lightning.

Angela hadn't come back to me the next morning, and now, due to the bitter necessity of food, we were sitting over omelets and pie in Ma's Friendly Hut in a run-down village called Star Lake. The irony of it struck me and I laughed inside, trying to keep my face blank.

"Ma!" a boy leaned in the door and shouted. "Lolly," he said, "tell Ma a phone call."

I watched a small ancient woman emerge from the kitchen behind Lolly and go outside to the pay phone pinned to the wall beside the plate window.

"Ma," I said, jerking my thumb at the woman and grinning at Angela, who refused to share even that with me. I gave up. The hell with her. "Let's go," I said.

Angela slid, wordless, from the booth and went out, while I paid the tab and slid the change onto the table.

"Thanks," the waitress called. "You all come see us again, now."

I waved and left. A station wagon drew up behind my car with a deer roped fender to fender on its roof. The deer's throat was slit and gaping; its eyes were glassy yet almost surprised as though some law of nature had suspended itself for no reason. I stood on the curb, staring at it, digging out my keys.

"What'er you gaping at?" the man climbing out of the car said.

"Hey, Hube." The waitress had sneaked out behind me.

"Help me get this here spike off the car, will you?" Hube said to her.

I was bothered by that deer as I drove off, but I couldn't figure out why. Finally, I exclaimed to Angela, "A doe." No wonder the animal looked surprised.

Angela reached down and changed the station on the radio.

"You don't care, I know. But don't you see? It's illegal. Once laws are broken like that, there's no telling. Hunters!"

"Men," Angela said.

"Oh, come on. Give me a break. You just grouped me in with guys like Hube back there."

"Yep," she said.

"Damn." I didn't yell. I squeezed the wheel, measuring the strength of my grip. "You know, if you weren't so chicken, we could talk about whatever's still bothering you."

I changed the radio, trying to get a rise out of her, deciding at the same time that I despised these rolling hills. They never changed. They were always the same.

Angela calmly dialed the radio back to her station.

"Is it still the fact that I yelled at you? I said I was sorry."

I waited.

"Please, Angela." I turned the radio down. "Tell me."

"That," she said. "Other things."

"Like what?"

"Like why did you want them to know we were sleeping together?"

"What? Who?"

"The Mallorys. Why did you want them to know we were sleeping together?"

We were almost out of the mountains by now. The broad curving road had grown flatter, straighter, while I had grown more confused. "I don't know what you're talking about," I said.

"When we checked in. When Mrs. Mallory asked if we needed linens for one or two beds and you said one. You said, 'I guess they don't know we're sleeping together.'"

"I said that to *you*. Not Mrs. Mallory."

"Why?"

"It was a joke. I mean, it was just one of those things one says." I tried to explain that it was an intimacy, a meaningless joke which said, "I'm happy and in love with you and it amuses me that strangers don't seem to recognize how much in love we are." I made a mess of it.

All she replied was, "I won't be anyone's whore."

"You're not a whore," I said.

"And I won't be insulted. Called names."

My head spun. I was dizzied by the way the conversation kept jagging into twists and turns. I felt—what?—like pounding the dashboard with my fists, and I fantasized for a moment that I understood her husband's frustration; while I resented this burden he'd passed on to me, I also pitied him. No man has charts for these things.

"Another thing," Angela said as we stood on the front steps to her apartment. "I don't want to sleep with you for a while. I don't feel like I know you anymore, and I want time to get to know you."

I was beaten. All I could say was, "Do you want to go to the party tomorrow? We were invited."

"No."

"How about the night after? Want to go to a show?"

"Maybe," she said.

"Do you still want to see me?" I said, expecting her to laugh.

"Yes. Just less of you."

YOU KNOW WHAT? I AM STILL IN LOVE WITH HER—IN SPITE OF EVERYthing I've failed to comprehend.

At the party, which I went to alone, I talked about Angela to my best friend, knowing I probably shouldn't but knowing as well that I had to talk to someone and I could trust him.

"One of you is crazy" is all he said.

I couldn't understand. It was like trying to paint by the numbers on a canvas without any numbers. A splash of white here, a dot of ocher there. All I could decide was to give Angela a few days to think about things and then call me and say she missed me. I would tell her that I missed her—the truth—and that we could start over, work it out, and go on to be the ideal lovers we ought to have been.

Problem was, she never called. I waited a full week, thinking how maybe it was better to live in Star Lake where all that mattered was the opening day of deer season, and Angela never phoned. Maybe she called while I was out? I'd hardly gone out.

My hurt turned to angry pride and then the two ran together—angry hurt, like those colors running together on that canvas. Still she didn't call. I started to fear that her pride was preventing her, as mine had prevented me, though my original pride was now no more than embarrassment. And fear that she'd not missed me at all. Are women capable of that? Experience suggests one thing; facts, another.

I couldn't concentrate on my work and so, finally desperate, I wrote to her. "Oh Angela, my angel, why do we have to do this? Why can't we be true to one another?"

That was long ago—or at least it seems so. I got an unsigned note back, slipped under my door.

> I feel injured for having known you, and I deeply regret ever having let you follow me home from that party. I want only the courtesy people usually reserve for strangers or their favorite minority. You may assume I will do you no injury as long as you leave me in peace; but any effort, from this point on, to manipulate me or insult me further will be met with a wall of fire and your words will rebound on your own head.

I sat and wept in confusion when I read that—wept for Angela, for myself, and, yes, I confess it, for all the women and men gridlocked in this world of surprise and pain and broken laws.

Sometimes I dream I'm imprisoned in an invisible jail of my own making. Other times, I see the eyes of that doe tied to Hube's car and I know my best friend was right. One of us is crazy, and I think it's me because I still believe in love's forgiveness.

Sometimes, when that belief overwhelms me, I stand by the phone as though paralyzed, wanting to tell Angela—tell you, tell someone— that none of this is true. Would those words rebound on my head? What does *rebound* mean?

I dial her number at these times, and stop after the sixth digit.

I have a push-button phone, so it doesn't wear me out. What wears is holding the cradle of the receiver down with my index finger as if it's a trigger, listening to the silence, standing there lost and waiting, hoping for it to ring, knowing that even if it does, it's the end.

Talking Turkey, Not Goose

FOR A CHANGE, HE DECIDED, HE WOULD TRY MARRIAGE.

As he cast around, dipping his lines into streams shallow and deep, running and pooled, he knew he wanted to marry into a family as different as Dubrovnik from the tiny reservation in Washington state where he'd been raised.

Barron Gregs had experimented more than once with the free and easy life of living with women, convinced then that the marriage certificate was little more than a bureaucratic seal of society's approval, requiring you to prove that you could handle the details—blood tests, rings, ceremony—and a reception at which everyone you'd ever known came to drink and eat as much as possible to make up for the expense of the gift that they resented not a little at having to give to people they either did not or no longer did care for, not really. A droll affair, to say the least, at which you and your bride got drunk to alleviate the humiliation and boredom that came from having to listen to the double entendres, puns, and witticisms made at your expense.

And he had liked, for the time being, living with these women, the way in which you could avoid having to participate—"put up with," he said—in their families. Their families tended to leave the two of you alone, some of them suspicious over your unwillingness to endure the legalities of a wedding ceremony, all of them convinced that until the relationship was formalized, they need not take the living together seriously.

"It wouldn't last, probably," they said. "Or if it does, the kids will get married."

Some parents, like his own father, just pretended that he wasn't living with anyone at all, and thus, visits were limited in time and subject with him. His stepmother, Anna, pretended that the woman's clothes in the closet were a kind of convenience, a limitation of space in the house, and that she—whoever she was—actually slept in a separate bed, even in a separate bedroom, the way Anna did. His father merely hated them, perceiving the women he lived with to be harridans or harpies, in a similar way to her father, who looked at Gregs with the jealousy of a lover who has been always too shy to express his desires. 'You're ruining my daughter, destroying her reputation,' the fathers' looks seemed to say, 'And I know you'll move on, once she has served out her usefulness.' The looks of these fathers made him smile secretly. Yet they also made him uncomfortable. He always wanted to prove to the father that he loved the daughter—and was being merely uncooperative by not providing the only proof the father would accept.

Still, despite the discomfort when he was around her parents or she was around his, living together unmarried eased the problems of holidays. Thanksgivings, for example, he would resign himself to enduring his own family which didn't really celebrate the invasion of the Pilgrims but used the holiday to get together and eat. She would spend the weekend with hers. The High Holy Days, Christmas, or Easter (depending on her family's religion) were the same: she was free to go home, and he was free. If she questioned his refusal to marry, he would ask her what difference a piece of paper made, and for a long time, he believed that the only difference it could possibly make was to make you feel constrained.

"Choice," he liked to say, "matters. If we're not married, then every day, I have to choose again to live with you, and that should say more than all the legal certificates in the world."

He said this to Julie Askew, a girl from work whom he'd been pursuing with the self-imposed patience that came from having lived with women, and from the fact that Julie was a good deal younger than he. He assumed, in his steaming patience, that he would, most likely, end up living with Julie and that, after a probationary period of, say, two years—an allotment of time that expanded and contracted with the temperature of his patience—he would marry her and settle down for good.

Certain events conspired to change his mind. Sent to London on business for two months, the British efficiency of the Royal Mail managed to keep any of Julie's letters from him for the first month, delivering a packet of them all at once, in the fifth week. By then, he had already had time to wonder if Julie hadn't taken his lectures on choice a little too much to heart.

His half brother, Harry, flew to London to visit him, where they spent the evenings walking and talking in defense against the British anti-Americanism which Harry coined *their peninsular xenophobia*. Harry had just gone through his third divorce, the difference being, as he said, that this one wasn't bitter.

"It just petered out," Harry said. "We're still friends," Harry added blithely, a phrase uncomfortably close to Julie's saying that she and Gregs would, no matter what, always be friends.

And it was in the Tate Gallery, standing before a large Clifford Still painting which he particularly liked, that Harry had said, "I don't marry them so I can understand them. I marry them so I can learn to live with them," and Gregs suddenly understood that there was little difference between his living with women and Harry's marrying them. Regardless of alimony, you could pay in either case. Certainly, Julie had made him pay usuriously for his age and his patience. Moving over to look once again at the confused order of the Jackson Pollock painting, Harry said, "Nothing's forever."

Regardless of what Harry meant, it was with the red slash of the Clifford Still painting yet in his visual memory, looking at the Pollock which he liked almost as much, that he knew for the first time in his life that what he wanted was that permanence that wasn't forever, that slash of red against the blue background, that yellow to balance it, the completeness of what, in the Pollock, might have begun as random and accidental lines—and which, in any other painting by any other painter, would have remained disordered.

He had his doubts about Julie Askew.

Besides, he was bored, in London. How many women he had known in his life went untotalled. But it was in London, also, that he had slept with a woman for purely sexual reasons, without jealousy on her or his part, without any of the words a couple uses to convince themselves there is something more than sex between them—just pure physical satisfaction—and he decided calmly and reasonably that life simply could not come only to this.

Harry had returned home two weeks ahead of him, two weeks in which he spent every free hour in that same room in the Tate, trying to comprehend the risks of Still's red, the permanent impermanence of Pollock's squiggle.

When he got home to New York, there was a telegram from Harry: "Father died(stop) Painless(stop) Letter follows(stop) Will delay wedding until Spring(stop)". The same day in his mailbox, there was a postcard from the woman in London saying she might be coming to New York and she would look him up, if she did. The last sentence ended in a question mark, as though she wondered if he'd want her to do so.

That night, he tossed and turned briefly, remembering the peculiar texture of her smoky skin and the secret thrill he had felt in touching it, the way a poor child might touch something in a department store that he knew couldn't afford. The next day, he changed his telephone number and gladly accepted the extra charge the phone company imposed for not listing his name in the public directory.

So it was, in that peculiar state of mind in which the first half of one's life is severed from the second half, parentless (his real mother had died in childbirth), his hassle-free solitude drained of its comfort, that he began to look beyond Julie.

Cautious, at first, because he knew, as he repeatedly told himself, that he wasn't his usual rational self, a fact of which he was reminded each time another form from his father's lawyer arrived in the mail asking for his co-signature.

Harry flew in from Seattle on business. They talked of their father, he asked after his stepmother's health, Harry told him about his newest fiancé, and then Harry flew back to Washington State. He was happy for Harry, and some of his half brother's anticipation couldn't help but rub off onto him. Still, nothing. He went to concerts and movies, spent days sitting in the park talking half heartedly with Julie or a few other women who attracted him but, in always agreeing with whatever he said, made him wonder if his solitude wasn't a necessary condition or whether anticipation, excitement weren't a feeling he had outlived. A few times, he ended up in bed with these other women (never with Julie), more because it was expected of him, and always with this little voice at the back of his mind telling him that this was no risk at all.

In more than one instance, he slipped and called them by the name of the girl in London and, while he felt bad about slipping that way and hurting their feelings, he didn't care, not really.

The same kind of ennui affected him at work. At lunch, in the cafeteria subsidized by all of the companies in the building where you could get a really good sandwich for very little money, he was used to being joined by several of the women who worked in various departments. Single women, most of whom were attractive in one way or another. While he enjoyed the company of these women, the fact that they tended to sit with him and not with other men who worked for the company, unless the men, too, joined their table, didn't impress him with himself. Neither did it swell his ego; in fact, he rather liked other, younger men to eat with him because the women were young, girls really (he had wondered, off-handedly, when girls became women—at what moment in their lives did they emerge from the ashes of their girlhood to become adults?), and he could express his attraction to these girls by saying to one of the younger men, "If I were younger, I think I'd be interested in so-and-so." He didn't notice how often he said this sort of thing. Nor did he realize that to the men he liked, he had begun to say, "If I were ten years younger, I'd ask Mary out."

One day, after the girls had returned to work, he said this to Bob Edgerman, one of the newer luncheoners, and Edgerman replied, "Immaculate Mary?"

He gave Bob an inquisitive look, raising his eyebrows slightly.

"We call her that because of the way she spotlessly keeps to herself." He added, "If you know what I mean," and winked.

He did understand what Edgerman meant, but he didn't agree. Having been to Florence several times, he had grown tired of the innumerable "Enthroned Madonnas," nativities, and births of the virgin. And while this Mary dressed somewhat like those madonnas, in loose-fitting clothing, and her face had the unscarred innocence of the gently smiling mother of Christ, Mary's clothes seemed less intended as a way to hide her sex and more a matter of comfort. When she walked across the cafeteria with her tray in hand, she seemed clumsy, as though the tray threw her balance off, and sometimes she would stumble or spill. But when she walked away, with nothing foreign encumbering her, her walk seemed not what he would have called sexy, but very, very comfortable, as though her clothes were as happy with her walk as she seemed confident with her person.

And her smile, he decided because of that, was less innocent and more disinterested, except while she ate. Then her face was animated and she chewed exaggeratedly as though squeezing every last dram of flavor out of the food before she swallowed. Clearly, she enjoyed eating in a way the Enthroned Madonna had never had the chance to.

Evidently, Mary had a reputation for the way she dressed. "Like a hippy from Jersey," Edgerman said on another day. "It's been suggested to her more than once that she should dress more appropriately to someone who works in fabric design. With little change, as you can see, " Bob said, cutting his smile short because he spotted Mary stumbling towards the table, her tray in hand.

While Gregs believed that the company should interfere as little as possible in the lives and styles of its employees, he couldn't deny that the company paid, in part, for the employees to look their best, especially girls who worked in design where buyers visited, and could easily be disaffected by any lack of smoothness or stylishness. Clearly, Mary's mode of dress could turn a buyer off—buyers were picky people—yet Gregs still had to admit that he liked the way she dressed, and he especially liked the way she had ignored the more-than-implicit suggestions which must have been made to her repeatedly.

"Still," Edgerman said after lunch, picking up the conversation where he had been forced to leave it for the sake of decorum. "Still, she gets along with that Laura Popowitch, as testy and demanding as Popowitch is. She must be good at her job, which is why she hasn't been fired for those ridiculous outfits. Either that, or, as some of the guys think, she's a lesbo."

Gregs surprised himself at the way he jumped up, like someone who has sat on a hassock with rebellious springs which give him a push as he rises, and said, "Excuse me. I've got to get back."

"See you around," Edgerman said. "Let me know what you find out."

"Yeah," he said. "Sure." He didn't intend to find out anything, he thought, as he wandered off down the corridor.

He felt irritated, and the corridor seemed empty, the atmosphere of hurry and the joy of profits noticeably absent, even though most people could be seen working, through the glass walls that separated the corridor from their offices. Even through the beige curtains, their attitudes, as they sat on stools over drawing tables or moved from one desk to another, seemed vague and undefined, lost a little, like children seem after a month of unrelieved vacation. Fall, Gregs thought. Because the company did little with wools, Fall was a dull time after the rush of summer sales, a time for calmly re-imagining last year's designs, re-evaluating last year's efforts.

At the end of the corridor, instead of turning for the elevators, he did something unexpected and turned right toward the set of rooms that were Popowitch's office, the design and layout rooms, and the small room with bolts of sample cloth stored on metal shelves.

Mary was inside. When she looked up from a layout table and said, "Hi. Can I do something for you?" he felt awkward and shy. He had hardly ever spoken alone to her, despite all the times she had joined his table at lunch, and he had no idea of what her ideas and attitudes were. In short, he didn't know what to say.

"Just thought I'd have a look around," he said. "I don't have much to do, upstairs," he said, regretting instantly having said "upstairs" because it sounded hierarchical.

Mary smiled, apparently not having noticed what he regretted. "Let me know," she said, and went back to what she'd been doing when he came in.

In the storage room, he pulled bolts of cloth out from their shelves and looked at them, aware that he knew almost nothing about the design of prints. He walked slowly up and down the short aisles, using up time until he thought he could leave without seeming uninterested.

"Like anything?" Mary said, her back to him, as he was sneaking out. She was rinsing a squeegee for silk-screening in the stainless steel sink.

"One or two," he said.

"Show me," she said, drying her hands and crossing the room. She led him into the storage room.

"This one, I like," Gregs said, touching a bolt of brightly colored fabric.

"You're so wrong!" she exclaimed, laughing. "You'd look like a peacock, in a dress made out of that."

Somewhat taken aback, but not resentful, Gregs pointed to another bolt. "How about that one?" he asked.

She laughed again, taking pleasure in the laughing the way she seemed to take pleasure in eating. Strangely, Gregs didn't feel that she was laughing at him, but that she was enjoying the imagined vision of a woman dressed in the colors he'd selected.

"No. You don't," she said. Controlling her laughter, she said, "You have to imagine what these would look like on a woman as a dress or a skirt. Those would look either garish, or dull. Too loud and too quiet. Dull in a loud way," she added, as though it was a private joke. To him, she said, "You've got to imagine these on a model, looking exquisite, and yet tasteful. Exquisite, in order to attract the attention of the women sitting in the fashion show's audience; tasteful, because it's the tastefulness that allows those same women to delude themselves and think they just might look as good as the model in those particular colors or that design." She gave him a knowing look. "Boy, am I glad you don't design my clothes!" she said, laughing again.

And Gregs laughed too, thinking about the reputation of her clothes. "Maybe you're right," he said. "I guess what looks good in a storage room wouldn't look good on someone. Well," he said, leaving, "thanks."

"Any time," Mary said.

He forgot about the incident as Thanksgiving approached like a warning of the Christmas to follow when, for a few brief weeks, the company would bustle with parties and decorations, a few sales of the items that had been suitable for winter weather, and the inevitable rumors about having to lay people off—which seemed to go hand-in-hand with the end of the year and the sentimentality that surrounded Christmas.

Thanksgiving would have been Gregs's father's birthday and so, as it approached, the arthritic mood that pervaded the corridors seemed to attack him like a virus. He had thought that the shock of his father's sudden death would be the most difficult time, and that the pain would wear off. He had found otherwise, that the truly sad times were the first occasions, holidays, on which his father's absence would glare at him and arrest his mood, regardless of how hard he tried to maintain his equability. He had always disliked Thanksgiving, when he, like the other atoms of his family, would bombard the little town in Washington to consume ham or turkey and trimmings. He disliked it because, exhausted as everyone was, after the confusion and bickering of preparing a dinner large enough for twenty people, it would end badly with one brother yelling at another, a cousin screaming at her children, whatever—the unalterable tensions freed by the excuse of tiredness—and everyone would then return home to forget about what had happened, until the next year when each of them would wonder why they were becoming edgy and nervous, as Thanksgiving approached. He went, because he loved his father and he believed with a kind of religiosity that a son should be there on his father's birthday.

This year, as Thanksgiving came upon him, he learned that religious feelings don't die as easily as the icons; however, knowing that Thanksgiving Day's tensions would be awash with tears, self-accusations, and regrets, he postponed his trip out west until Christmas. He wanted to be alone, he told Harry, with their father's death, which had created inside of him what he could only describe as a void. It was an insistent absence, a vague dependence on a there which was there in its not-thereness (Gregs feared he was becoming philosophical; Harry feared his ends were loosening). It was, he told Harry before hanging up, akin to the feeling he'd had his first time overseas. With the ocean between, he was aware that he could not get home easily; dependent on someone else, strangers who ran airlines or American Express offices, he felt cut off from everything familiar.

At work, he thought he managed to disguise his feelings fairly well. Everyone knew of his loss, and everyone seemed willing to grant him extra patience when the mood surprised him like a mugger and he was short with them.

As Thanksgiving got nearer, a few people inquired what his plans were, and Julie insisted that he come to dinner with her family.

"You won't be imposing," she'd said at lunch. "Honest. My parents would love to have you."

"You're welcome to spend the day with the wife and kids," Edgerman said, thinking that perhaps Gregs didn't want to go to Julie's. "Nothing fancy, We're talking turkey, not goose," he said.

"Silly. Goose is for Christmas anyway," Julie said, and Gregs endured a wave of hatred for the propriety of Julie's life.

"Leave him alone," Mary said. She, herself, seemed taken aback by the way she said it, and her small mouth quivered as she tried to think of what to say next. "Listen," she said after another mouthful of food had been well-chewed and swallowed. "I . . . we," she looked around the table, including everyone, "are very sorry that your father died."

"Mary!" Julie hissed.

Mary returned Julie's glare with equal intensity.

"What the hay. I'm late. I've got to be going," Edgerman said.

After everyone but Mary had departed, Gregs sat there, wishing he could say something to erase the red from Mary's cheeks.

And later that afternoon, having thought about it in his office, he went downstairs to Popowitch's department, where he found Mary comparing color swatches. "These dyes," she said. "They're cheap. See? Like that tart, Julie," she added. She blushed and swallowed hard. She held up a swatch. "The colors don't take evenly. The first time this is washed, it's going to fade and streak."

"Thanks," he said, wondering why she had said that about Julie, feeling vaguely ashamed that he hadn't defended Julie and yet knowing that he did not care to defend her.

"For what?"

"For what you said at lunch. About my father. His dying."

"I'm sorry. I made everyone uncomfortable. I botch everything up. I meant . . .

"No," he said, interrupting her. "Really. I appreciate it." And he did. Thinking about the way her bald statement drove everyone from the table, he realized that at least part of his discomfort at work had been exactly that everyone seemed to know his father had died recently, and yet everyone seemed to try to ignore it. He had been left in uncertainty; not wanting pity, he could have used some sympathy, but he had been afraid even to mention the fact for fear that he would be depressing the people around him. Now, at least, it was out in the open, and he felt disburdened of a portion of his grief by having it that way.

"I just can't imagine what I would do," Mary said. "If my father died. Or my mother. I . . . ," she began to blush again, swallowing with little rapid swallows, as if she would cry or as if she wanted to withdraw what she was saying. "I love them so much. My daddy . . ."

"I loved my daddy, too," Gregs said. "A lot." Gregs couldn't help but smile, as he rode the elevator back up to his office. He had loved his father. For that, he felt lucky.

II.

THANKSGIVING CAME AND WENT. ON THANKSGIVING DAY, GREGS WAS too depressed to do anything but open a can of tuna fish and force himself to eat it on crackers. He listened to Harry, over the phone, and spoke once to Julie Askew, who kindly called to re-invite him to dinner.

"It's not too late," she said, "to change your mind."

"I've already eaten," he said. "Come over for dessert, then," Julie said.

"I wouldn't be much fun," he said. "But thanks, anyway?"

The day after Thanksgiving, Gregs decided to get out of the house. It was the Christmas season. Determined to win out over the crowds and the fluorescent claustrophobia he felt in department stores and do his shopping, he ended up in the Frick Museum. Heading straight for Turner's *The Harbor of Dieppe*, he ran into Mary. Tilting her head thoughtfully, concentrating on the Constable facing the Turner, she failed, at first, to notice him.

"Hi," he said, unintentionally sneaking up behind her and causing her to jump.

"Oh!" she said. "It's you. You frightened me."

"Sorry," he said, laughing.

She whirled and crossed towards the Turner. He followed. She took a step or two away from him, and focused on the painting.

"I prefer the Turner," he said.

Glancing surreptitiously around the room like a successful thief or a terrorist about to kidnap Turner for ransom, she said, "I like the Constable," and crossed the room, again.

Gregs felt that she didn't want to be seen with him. Had she come to the museum with someone? Talking to a man you knew from work didn't seem a cause for jealousy, so again he followed her. For a minute, their contrary migrations stopped, and he stood near her in the center of the room while she explained sketchily why she preferred the Constable.

"There are some wonderful Constables in London. Several of them have this dog, the same dog, but always in a different posture. I've always liked that dog."

He felt silly because she didn't reply. He worried that by mentioning London he might have sounded as though held one-upped her somehow, so quickly he added, "Of course, maybe you're right. Maybe this Constable is a better painting, as painting goes."

She looked up at him and smiled, a small smile, as though she were about to challenge him on that phrase, "as painting goes," tilting her head in an unusual way, like someone who's had a mild case of polio might do, or someone who had a crick in her neck.

"On the other hand," she said, "maybe you're right to like the Turner."

He decided then that he liked the way she smiled although, as with the paintings, he couldn't say exactly why.

"So," Mary said. "How was your Thanksgiving?"

With any other girl, he would have been sure that she was asking whom he'd spent Thanksgiving with. With Mary, however, he wasn't so sure. "Quiet," he replied.

"What did you have, for dinner?" she asked.

"Tuna fish," he said. "On crackers."

While it was true, he had meant this to be funny. Her jaw hardened and her eyes looked quickly away. It was obvious that his remark hadn't struck Mary as funny.

"Well," she said. "I've got to go."

"I'll walk out with you." She looked at him, making him add, "If that's all right."

She shrugged, helplessly. "Well. . . . I've got to find someone."

He felt awkward, following her into another room, and yet he was curious, too. She went up to a man in a baggy sweater, who was standing before Duccio's *Temptation of Christ*, and slipped her hand into the crook of his elbow. When the man turned his head towards her, Gregs knew instantly that this was her father. Their noses were identically Roman, although hers ended in the hint of a button, while his seemed to emphasize the length of his face.

"Isn't that beautiful, Dolly?" her father asked her, nodding at the Duccio.

Gregs looked, too. He had never much cared for Trecento Italian painting. Rather, he had difficulty in finding the beauty in so many religious subjects and this one was small, its colors faded.

"Look at this line," her father said, tracing a curve from Christ, down through the fortified buildings bottom right and over to the buildings on the left. He shoved his hands deep into the pockets of his trousers and tilted his head. "It's almost as wonderful as a Giotto," he added, and from the way he said it, Gregs believed it had to be. In fact, in his awkwardness, Gregs felt that he was seeing for the first time something to admire in these paintings.

"Daddy," Mary said. "I want you to meet someone."

Her father seemed to shrink into himself, like a crustacean tentatively pulls its head back, ready to recede entirely into its shell if the possible threat proves actual.

"This is Barron Gregs. Barron, my father."

"How do you do?" Gregs said, thrusting his hand out, ready to shake hands firmly, the way he had always imagined fathers liked men who knew their daughters to shake hands.

Her father managed to pull a hand from his pocket and shake Gregs's hand, but in a way that instantly told Gregs not to squeeze too hard. Gregs noticed, too, that the man's fingers were short, the palms of his hands fleshy. Not fat, but fleshy, like Mary's—something he'd noticed before but never consciously recognized.

"Glad to meet you," her father said diffidently, looking briefly at Gregs's eyes and then quickly away at his daughter. Gregs remembered Mary's saying how much she loved her father and he thought he could see in the father's eyes an equal love, an unbridled affection and gentleness that, had they not been father and daughter, would have given Gregs a twinge of jealousy. As it was, he felt a bit envious: at her age, he would never have exchanged such a look with his own father, and she had. He had always assumed that, by a certain age, children and parents outgrow such open affection.

"Are you ready to go, Dadski?" Mary said.

"Sure, Dolly," he said. "Just let me get my coat."

As they exited on to the street, Gregs said, "I was supposed to be Christmas shopping today. Guess I didn't get it done. Obviously. I hate shopping, don't you?"

"I don't mind it. Unless it's for myself. For other people, I don't mind, though."

He turned left at the bottom of the steps.

"Well," she said, "We go this way. See you."

He watched her for a minute, intrigued by the way her long strides seemed not heavy or graceless, but not graceful, either, amused by the indifference of her cotton skirt and baggy sweater which seemed, at best, mismatched. Her father wore an old wool over-coat and kind of scuttled along beside her. "I can see where she gets her style of dress," Gregs thought, smiling. He turned for home.

He forgot about it. He was used to forgetting brief encounters, and this hadn't even been an encounter. Still, on Tuesday next, as he stood at the cosmetics counter in Macy's buying perfume for Harry's fiancé, he was discomfitted by the hard eyes of the salesgirl, eyes made large and mean by mascara and eyeliner; and he was irritated by her tight-fitting suit and the white silk blouse that hid with ruffles the skin it had been designed to expose. He felt a vague anger over the salesgirl's deference to his money, and by the time she asked him if there would be anything else, he could barely manage a polite "No" through clenched teeth.

This anger, he found, carried over into Wednesday when he snapped at Julie Askew because of her deference to his position with the firm. "You don't like my ideas on this project," he said. "So why the hell are you pretending?"

She had looked stricken, her face betraying a mixture of confusion and rage.

"I'm sorry," he apologized. "I don't seem to be myself, today." To make it up to her, he treated her to dinner, during which he was privileged to learn how often his assistants had not agreed with him, recently, and he decided to seek and pay attention to their ideas with greater openness.

They went to see a movie, after which they went for coffee, and he made the obligatory passes at Julie, which she still had the good sense to turn down. Gregs wondered, momentarily, if he was slipping noticeably into middle age, but decided that no, Julie did enjoy his company a lot, but she was being as cautious as he was. No matter what, they would be good friends. That was okay with Gregs.

On Friday, he ate lunch, and found himself looking around at the people grouped at tables with their trays of food. He hadn't seen Mary since the Frick. Edgerman asked him if he was going to the office Christmas party the next week and, looking at Julie and smiling, Gregs said he wouldn't miss it. Leaving Edgerman behind to wonder why he had smiled so at Julie, he wandered off down the corridor. It felt empty, unbusy to him, and he knew it was because of the insistence of the employees on taking all of the lunch hour, which had been pared down to forty-five minutes in the effort to economize. Through the glass doors, he saw Mary, eating a sandwich from a brown paper bag, as she leaned on her stool and gazed out the windows at the skyline. She stood, looked down at something happening in the park across the street, and then sank back into her revery on the stool. He decided to go in and have a look around. As he opened the door and Mary looked around at him, still chewing her sandwich, he felt, for the first time in years, timid. Had she not already seen him and smiled, he would have let the doors close and sneaked back down the hall to the elevators.

"Hi," Mary said. He nodded, unable to say as much as a hello. "What's up?" she asked, giving him an inquiring look because he was just standing there, trying not to slump into his timidity.

"Nothing. I haven't seen you in a while. I was wondering what happened to you. Tired of the lunchtime crowd?"

He was about to chuckle, but stopped, as she said, "Sort of." She waved her sandwich at nothing in particular. "I've felt like being alone. Thinking."

"About anything special?"

She shook her head, turning back to the window.

"Well," he said. He stood there, not knowing what to say next, feeling how useless hands were, how awkwardly they hung in the air at the ends of one's arms. He mumbled that he ought to be going, but he didn't make a move. Finally, he asked, "Are you coming to the Christmas party?"

"I doubt it," Mary said, abruptly. "I don't really like parties. People do such silly things."

"True," he said, not realizing how true it would be. Still, it might be fun." He got as far as the door. "Listen," he said. "Maybe. . . . Remember how you said you didn't mind shopping? Maybe you'd go shopping with me, before Christmas, help me get it done? I need help. If you wouldn't mind? If you give me your address, maybe I could give you a call?"

"Sure," she said, brightening. She wrote on a scrap of paper her phone number and address, and handed it to him, smiling. "Don't lose it," she said.

"I won't." He couldn't help smiling back at her. And when he left, he felt lifted, happy. Mary seemed to be such a contradiction, at one moment anti-social, the next, willing to endure a day's shopping with him. What had she meant when she'd said, "Don't lose it"? Maybe I won't go to the party, either, he thought, knowing that in his position, he was obliged to go.

"Howdy, Jules," he said as he got off the elevator, making her look at him, surprising her with his comraderie. "You going to the party this weekend?"

"Of course," she said. What she said next was cut off, as he entered his office and shut the door.

Gregs didn't lose Mary's number. He even tried to dial it a few times, but hung up before her phone had the chance to ring. He didn't have time for shopping; nor did he feel like doing so. The days between obtaining her phone number and the office party were not so much busy as depressing. The economic forecast for the next year was in, and the company was requiring each division to trim away fat, a euphemism which meant that each division head had to lay off two employees. Gregs didn't like the job, and he liked it even less around Christmas time. He imagined having to hand out pink slips to the selected employees at the party, like prizes after pinning the tail on the donkey, a simile, he told himself, that didn't fit, since he was the donkey. Or rather, the selected few were the donkeys, whose tails he would be cutting off. It didn't work.

Still, Gregs had his belief in choice to hold him together. He had chosen this job, and the unpleasant as well as the pleasant tasks were a part of it. He didn't like it much, but that's the way it was. Julie's job was one of the ones in question, though, and he felt he owed her something; even though she had never quite succumbed to his advances, she had endured them. But that didn't seem right. Fortunately, Julie was very good at her job, and he could probably justify laying off someone else instead of her. But was that fair? Was he, because he liked her, ranking her above someone who was equally good at his job?

He decided to postpone making any decisions until after Christmas. He couldn't have a good time, smile and be pleasant to people whose lives he was about to change; he could have a better time—as could they—if he wasn't looking at some of them as though they were about to be executed.

On top of this, problems had arisen about his father's estate. His father had written a will, unfortunately for his stepmother, that presumed they would both live to a ripe old age, and much of the estate was willed to the children. Personally, Gregs thought it fitting that the children simply agree to alter the effect of the will—that he and Harry and his half sister make over a large portion of their inheritances to his stepmother, with stipulations that any remainder go to the grandchildren. One of Harry's former wives didn't agree, though, and she was suing the estate for money that she claimed was rightfully hers. Lordy.

By the end of an hour's long-distance conversation with Harry, Gregs was thoroughly perturbed. Harry was whining, and Gregs, having his own problems, had said, "Look, Harry. If you didn't marry every bitch in heat, these problems wouldn't even occur. Go over to her house and knock her around a bit, why don't you? You should have done it a long time ago."

He slammed the phone down, and made himself a triple scotch which he drank most of, before he called Harry back and apologized, telling Harry about having to lay-off at least two people and probably three from his department at work. "At Christmas," he said. "Of all the cheerful seasons."

"You can refuse," Harry said, gaining control of his voice.

"It's my job, Harry," Gregs said.

"You could quit, couldn't you?" Harry was just like he was, at times. When he asked what good that would do, Harry had replied, "Remember what Dad used to say?" As though Gregs didn't remember, he said, "Never at the expense of labor. Make changes, Barron, economize, do your job. But never at the expense of labor. That's what Dad would tell you."

It was unfair. His father had been a union organizer way back when things were simple, and it didn't seem quite fair to Gregs for his half brother to throw this in his face, now.

As he dressed for the party, he kept drinking, trying to put himself in the mood for a party. He knew he would fail, but with each rush of the booze, he cared less and less.

He arrived late and remembered little. He remembered that he had been rude to Edgerman because Edgerman had raised the question of lay-offs, saying that in his department the problem wasn't who to lay-off but who to keep.

Mary had come to the party after all and, drunk as he was, he sat down near her. The way she had turned her whole body, rotating her shoulders as well as her head and said "Hello" had frightened him. He knew he was drunk and, surprised by her warmth, he didn't want to be drunk in front of her. The double dimples formed on her cheeks by her smile embarrassed him, and he got up and left the room.

He left very early, accompanied by Julie Askew, who wasn't going to let him try to find his way home without help; and the next morning, Julie was kind enough to say that she'd been drunk too, and that, as far as she was concerned, this didn't mean things had changed between them.

"I felt sorry for you," she said. "You seemed so alone."

He felt an abiding gratitude towards her tact, as he took her home. He hated himself for wondering if he had mentioned the lay-offs to her, and if that was why she had slept with him. Every time he'd opened his eyes and looked at her, laying there beneath him, perhaps with pleasure but without enjoyment, he had seen not Julie's but Harry's first wife's face. It carried him back to the way he had felt in London, the summer before, and he realized that for her sake, if not for his, it was over between him and Julie. By sleeping together, they had removed the only unknown left, and it had been that unknown that had made either of them wonder if they could be more than friends. They would remain friends, but the friendship would never quite be the same again—and he both regretted that and was glad of it. Glad, because one problem was removed from his life. Another took its place.

He was ashamed of himself. He didn't know if he could face anyone at work—especially not Mary. It had always been a rule of his never to become intimate with someone who worked for him, and a good rule it was. He might take them out for an evening, even make half-hearted passes at them, but as long as they worked for him, he had managed to maintain a respectable flirtatiousness. He was so adamant in this that, especially combined with the repeated urgings and temptations he'd felt over the years, he had fired a man just under him for sleeping with his secretary. It was a matter of power, and even though he understood that a certain amount of flirtation went on between men and women who worked together, he had been taught by his father that power had to be used maturely and fairly. To step over the boundaries was the first step towards the complete perversion of power.

Now, he had done it, stepped over, and even though Harry suggested that he might learn something from it and never do it again, he wasn't sure he could. How was he to trust himself? Next time he was drunk, would he use that as an excuse to do the same thing?

"Forgive yourself," Harry said at the end of one of his pained and worried phone calls.

That night, Gregs's dreams made *Rosemary's Baby* look like *Bambi*.

For three days, he called in sick. Sooner or later, he would have to face it, but he wanted to understand it, first. The only times he left his house were to shop for food, to pick up cigarettes—a habit he returned to out of self-hatred, having quit successfully two years before. For those three days, he stayed in bed and tried to read. Words passed in front of his eyes, and he turned pages. He remembered nothing of what he read. He watched icicles drip from the eaves and imagined them growing huge like clear teeth of a prehistoric monster. Finally, he slunk back to work, still faced with the job of laying off employees.

No one mentioned the party and at first he was relieved. Maybe he hadn't made such an ass out of himself as he'd imagined. He apologized to Edgerman who said there was no need for an apology. Rather, Edgerman was grateful that Gregs had jumped on his too cavalier attitude towards the lives of people who worked for him. That made Gregs feel a bit better. Julie behaved towards him in the same way she had before the party: she was neither cold nor overly warm, and the one time he said, "Julie, listen, I . . . ," she'd said, "Forget about it. I know."

He imagined that he felt a new and special admiration, not for Julie alone, but for womankind. Still, he continued to stay away from the cafeteria.

Friday, after booking plane reservations to Seattle, he was on the phone to Harry, telling him what time to pick him up at the airport, when Mary knocked and entered his office without being asked. "I've got to go, Harry," he said.

Hanging up the phone, he looked at her. She looked straight back at him, a sliver of sarcasm at either corner of her mouth.

"What can I do for you?" he asked in as business-like tone as he could muster.

"I was wondering where you've been," she said. "Figured you were hiding out. After the party . . ."

"I've been busy," he said. He fiddled with papers and pencils on his desk, avoiding her eyes. Thoughts darted through his mind like roaches surprised by light. Gregs was not a little irritated by the way she felt free to walk right into his office, let alone mention the party, and yet, secretly, he was relieved and happy to see her again.

"Uh huh," Mary said. "Sure. After all, this is the busy season, isn't it?"

"Listen . . ."

"So," Mary said. "Everyone was surprised by you and that slut, Julie, at the party. The way you left." She chuckled. "Susan Hackert kept telling everybody that she couldn't believe it. Stephanie sat in a corner, weeping." She laughed. "You caused quite a stir among the women folk."

Gregs didn't know what to say. Should he deny it? Protest? That wouldn't fool Mary. He waved his hands in a half-excusatory shrug.

"Well," Mary said. "I just stopped in to see how you were. I'll go." At the door, she stopped, and asked, "Tell me, did you enjoy it?"

He thought he was going to tell her that it was none of her business, perhaps even say he was sorry, try to explain, claim drunkenness, et cetera. At least try to dispel some of the discomfort he felt at Mary's directness. He had never been good at talking about such things, not with women, and especially not with women he liked—and most especially when he knew he was in the wrong. He looked at her by the door.

The sarcasm seemed to be there, still, and yet he couldn't find a trace of bitterness or hatred, unless, perhaps, it was in the way her chin doubled, slightly, as she lowered her head to stare at him. Each time he opened his mouth and tried to speak, the words caught in his gullet. The effect made him look like a fish in an aquarium or one of those elderly ladies who silently work their mouths open and closed over a row of slots in Vegas.

"Well, you have my phone number. Unless you've lost it," Mary said, and left.

Barron Gregs spent the greater part of that afternoon sharpening pencils after he'd broken off their points, testing the sharpness on the palms of his hands until it hurt, leaving his palms mottled, like the palms of someone with a fever or allergy. To say that he was confused would be an exceptionally commonplace way to put it. He had never met a woman who could be so matter-of-fact, let alone be willing to overlook such an incident. He had never imagined himself as worthy of that kind of forgiveness. Had he said anything about sleeping with Julie, he would have meant it as a clever lie, a way of avoiding the distinction between consummation and conclusion. The more he considered the matter, the more the incident ran together like watercolors on saturated paper with the woman in London of the summer before. As the afternoon wore on, the colors began to separate again: he recalled the vision of Julie's face when he had opened his eyes, and how it had not only looked passively astonished like Harry's first wife, but also hardened, solipsistically intent on deriving its own pleasure. It made him know that Julie, surprised by where she had come to be, was determined that as long as she was there, she would enjoy herself as best she could. Then, too, he had to confess to himself that he had been as solipsistic as she, concerned more with performance than with the clumsy but affectionate exchange of sensation.

When these separated colors of his thinking dried, they were harsh and distinct. He could have been any functioning male that night, and because of that, Julie could, in some sense of the word, be called a slut. And Gregs was too logical not to realize that the same applied to him. What was shame and embarrassment became, now, a kind of horror.

III.

BARRON GREGS'S HORROR RESULTED IN A KIND OF STASIS THAT HE TRIED to overcome by taking Mary shopping. His own version of wearing a hair shirt, doing penance, certain that he would have to listen to her mention the party and its aftermath innumerable times, and yet determined to endure it.

He awoke on Saturday morning from *Porgy and Bess* dreams in which he was the cripple, pulling himself around legless on his wheeled platform. Oddly, he wasn't depressed by the dreams. No, what hung over and impressed him most upon waking was the feeling of joy, in the dream, over how mobile he was, how strong were his arms and how supple his shoulders.

The day was uneventful, you might say even dull, except that by the end of the afternoon, he had finished all of his shopping. Walking around lower Manhattan, he had felt out of place because of the way he was dressed and he felt a peculiar pleasure in Mary's company, admiring her ability to find the nicest presents for the least amount of money. Gregs figured that shopping on his own the exact same presents would have cost him twenty percent more.

In Barnes and Noble, for example, buying the last available copy of a history of motion pictures for his stepmother, who loved movies, Mary had talked the manager into reducing the price because of an unimportant and hardly noticeable wrinkle in the binding. Gregs, himself, never would have done such a thing, and while he was as embarrassed as the manager was unprepared, he admired Mary all the more. He had always paid the price demanded without question and, he reflected, that willingness had carried over in to the way he had lived.

From time to time, Mary would point at a girl Gregs was staring at and call her something harsh like "slut" or "tart," and Gregs would set himself on edge, gathering his words like a sheaf of olive branches, preparing to alter the subject. Other times, Mary would say, "I saw the way that tart looked at you. She'd eat you alive."

Gregs, unaware not of the look he'd gotten but of its meaning, thought to himself how strange it was that women could interpret the subtle looks and odd gestures of other women—the same as he could do with men—while if she was right men had no idea what women meant by their glances and looks. It was as though each sex gave off the right signals, but for the wrong railroad.

In spite of her insistent criticism of every woman Gregs found attractive, Mary never once mentioned the party or Julie, though Gregs remained on the look-out for signals warning him to change the subject.

Around five, unwillingly, he took her home, where he met her mother and she reintroduced him to her father as though the Frick had never happened. He accompanied her upstairs out of courtesy and gratitude for not hearing about the party, even though he disliked meeting parents as much as, evident from the way her father shrank into himself at Gregs's entrance, her father disliked meeting or seeing him. Her mother's voice, asking how was shopping, was high, more energetic than Gregs would expect for such a commonplace question. "Bright would describe it," he told himself, taking in as many details as he could without gaping. The focus of the loft was a long table, illuminated, as it was, by a stained glass lamp which threw most of its light down, and not out, trapping the horizontal light in reds and yellows and slivers of green.

"Went fine," Gregs said.

Mary sat in a chair beside the oak table and removed her shoes. Gregs looked around, selecting a seat opposite to her and to her father's right, trying to make himself as unobtrusive as possible in the streaks of red cast by the lamp. The only other light in the room was from a fluorescent tube, buzzing noisily above the stove and sink, trying to divide its territory from that of the table.

Her father said little to him, really, so he kept his mouth shut, knowing from experience that fathers didn't always get along with their daughters' dates. In fact, no one, at first, said much to him. Mary immediately became involved in a discussion the father and mother were having, their voices at the volume of two people listening to the same walkman. Not shouting, exactly, but loud enough to hurt if your head ached.

"I tell you, we're talking turkey, here," Mary's father said. "It's Christmas. We always have turkey on Christmas. We don't have ham out of consideration for Avi, and we aren't having goose."

"I just thought . . . ," Mary's mother said.

"Well, don't," the father said. "You'll mess it up."

"If she wants to have goose, let her have goose," Mary said.

"Turkey," the father said.

The discussion went that way, the mother checking her list of what people were going to bring to dinner and claiming that goose would be nice with the expected side dishes and condiments, the father insisting that turkey was what they were talking, and Mary interjecting her opinions and advice. Only once or twice did Mary take notice of him, leaning across the table to say things like, "We always go through this," like stage directions which caused Gregs to nod, smile wanly, and, while wishing someone would offer him a drink, concentrate on placing the sound that came from the direction of the refrigerator. It sounded like a kitten learning to whistle.

At one point, his hopes for a drink were raised when the father pushed his empty glass towards Mary, who jumped up. "Coke?" she asked. He nodded his head, yes, without interrupting the argument over what the family and its friends were going to have for Christmas dinner.

"Mommy," Mary said, giving her father his refilled coke glass, "just have turkey. Otherwise, daddy . . . ," and Gregs felt off-base, piqued by Mary's giving her attention to her father, and not to him.

"Marriage," the mother, Betsy, said.

"What about marriage," the father said.

"It's an acquired taste," Betsy smiled and said to Gregs, "like Miracle Whip."

Gregs smiled, afraid to laugh.

In his own family, Gregs knew, a drink was the first thing you would offer someone and, if there were more than two members of the family gathered around the stranger, it would be followed by an immediate refill. A habit, built up over the years, aimed at sedating the nerves of the guest against the fighting which might break out at any moment. This family was different. For one, while his father had not been a weak man, he had never dominated a room the way Mary's father seemed to be able to do. Mary's father was a small, Rasputinish man, with eyes that you could only call wild or intense. Each time his eyes, which glistened like eyes about to cry, crossed the line of Gregs's vision, resting on Gregs momentarily, Gregs felt the power that emanated from him. His eyes had feeling, and it was this intuition that made Gregs believe that the father was ignoring him not out of jealousy, as much as out of simple shyness.

"Heart," Gregs told himself. He meant that the love in the room was a matter more of heart than reason. If Gregs had felt out of place walking around lower Manhattan with Mary, he definitely felt out of place here.

And yet, too, he felt comfortable. Not because of Mary—and he remained irritated by that, excusing it because she was so much younger. It was the mother, he realized, as he caught himself admiring her legs while she stood at the sink, who generated the feeling of welcome. Gregs could see where Mary got the slight button on her Roman nose, and he noticed that her mother had a similar ease of movement, except when she lifted a pot from the stove and carried it to the sink. It was the mother who, making herself a Bloody Mary, apologized for ignoring "their" guest, and gave him a drink, Seagrams, which was as close to bourbon as their eclectic liquor shelf could approximate. The brief exchange of pleases and thank you's interrupted the argument over turkey and goose, which, Gregs was immediately aware, was a mistake.

"So," her father said, looking off into the middle distance, "that was some Christmas party you people had."

Gregs froze, staring hard into his drink and watching the ice cubes melt under the heat transmitted by the hands he wrapped thoughtfully around the glass.

"Mary came home all upset, asking could we believe it, some boss had gone home with his secretary."

Gregs looked over at Mary for a sign as to whether her father knew which boss.

"You're such a bozo, sometimes," her father said to her. "How can you be so naive."

"He didn't just go home with her," Mary said, vehemently. "He porked her."

Evidently, Gregs thought, any topic was open to conversation in this family.

"Even if it was wrong, Dolly, human beings can make mistakes, you know."

"It's still wrong," Mary said, her vehemence subsiding—aimed, Gregs felt, less at him than at the act, itself.

"Have a talk with your boss," Betsy said. "That's one thing about Mary," she added to Gregs, "She can get these things off her chest and then forget about them. She's never been one to hold grudges."

"She somehow thinks it doesn't happen all the time," the father said, laughing.

"I hate you sometimes," Mary said, hurt by his laughter.

Gregs was startled.

"What do you think?" the father asked Gregs, still laughing.

"I think," Gregs began, trying to formulate an answer that would conclude the discussion. Fortunately, the doorbell rang and everything screamed to a halt as the father buzzed the arrival through the downstairs door and watched, as whoever it was climbed the stairs.

"I forgot to tell you," Betsy told Mary. "Jonathan was released from Bellevue yesterday. He's having dinner with us. Barron, you'll stay, too, of course?"

"Oh, I couldn't."

"How is he?" Mary asked.

"Does it matter?" her father said from the doorway. "It's the holidays, and we're not going to let him spend them alone."

"I was only asking," Mary said.

"He's okay," Betsy said. "I've seen him better, but I've seen him much worse, too."

Gregs understood this cryptic exchange after meeting Jonathan who presented Mary's parents with a bottle of wine. After asking several times where he should sit, wandering around the table like a child lost among the choices in a department store, and finally being told by Mary's father to sit anywhere, Jonathan took a seat across from Gregs. He proceeded to tell everyone about the wine—what region it was from in Spain, and what that meant about its bouquet and dryness. "It's a nouveau," Jonathan would say. "A young wine, which means it's fruitier, or so the owner of the liquor store I go to said . . . I only go to the owner, he's the only one I ask about wines . . . He knows his wines. Here, taste," he said, pouring an ounce or two into a glass. "What do you think? It's a new wine, you see. Young. It means it's been picked earlier and pressed into wine. . . ." Jonathan went on, repeating himself several times.

Mary, her father, and Betsy half ignored Jonathan, after listening to his initial explanation. They didn't seem to be ignoring him out of discomfort or dislike, but more out of tolerance, as one would ignore an insistent child that one loved. Gregs sniffed the bouquet of the bottle. It was thin and fruity, the way nouveaux are, as though it was something other than wine.

"I ask you," Jonathan said, "doesn't that smell fresh. It's a nouveau . . ."

Gregs nodded. It was an expensive wine that Gregs recognized, even though he did not care for nouveaux.

"It's very nice," Mary's father said.

"Here," Jonathan said, pouring some into another glass, and pushing the glass towards Gregs. "Tell me what you think."

It tasted the way Gregs imagined crushed grape flowers would taste, if there were such things. Thin and dry, and yet very fruity. A little too fruity, for Gregs's palate. He sensed that it was not necessary to honestly say what he thought of it, and he mimicked the father. "Very nice," he said, terrorized by the thought that it would have been useless to try to discuss the wine with Jonathan.

Gregs tried at first to follow Jonathan as Jonathan went from wine to D. H. Lawrence, to an opening in Soho, to something Gregs couldn't catch. It was like playing an electronic pursuit game, and Gregs wasn't any better at those. He gave up, content simply to observe as Jonathan puttered along. Every now and then, Jonathan, becoming aware that no one was listening, without altering his posture or the interiorized look of his eyes, would raise his voice to the level of pronouncement—always, Gregs noted, addressing the father.

"Déjà vu," Jonathan would say to himself. Then, "Tony, you know what déjà vu is?"

Tony would not say anything, and Jonathan would go on, raising his voice, saying, "Déjà vu. It's like going someplace again and thinking you've been there before."

Swallowing a solitary laugh, Gregs snorted like some rutting animal. He decided to finish his drink as quickly as possible without sucking it down, wishing that he was as at ease as Jonathan, hoping, at the same time, that he would continue to be overlooked.

"May I get you another?" Betsy asked him. "It's nice having someone to have a drink with."

"No thanks. I really do have to be going. I still have to pack, tonight." He stood, causing his chair to tip backwards, and blushed.

"No problem," Tony said, laughing. "Around here, things get dropped all the time. You can always tell what Mary's eaten by looking at what's on her clothes."

Gregs almost stumbled into saying, 'I know,' but caught himself. "It was nice meeting all of you," he said.

"Come back and watch the superbowl," Jonathan shouted after him.

He felt lucky to have escaped unscathed by the discussion of the party, and he was pleased that Mary denied having told her parents that he was the boss in question. He believed her. That months later she would confess that she had told her parents didn't matter. Even then, Gregs would believe that it had been a necessary lie, for his sake, done with the same intentions as Mary's father sending Jonathan to his dentist for minor surgery, and paying for it himself.

"So," he said to Mary, who had accompanied him down to the street level door.

"What did you think? About my family, or most of it anyway."

"Different,"Gregs said. He shuffled his feet, delaying leaving. "Maybe I'll see you when I get back?"

"Have a good trip," she said. "Think about me."

IV.

THESE WERE THE OTHER EVENTS WHICH CONSPIRED TO CHANGE GREGS'S mind, all of them revolving around Christmas, though each of them compartmentalized like the revolving doors at Macy's:

The night before he enplaned for Seattle—like so many nights in his future still to come—Barron Gregs came awake as if from dreaming, standing at attention at his bedroom window. He had been filled with imaginings of Mary doing everyday, common tasks—eating, drinking, talking, sleeping—aware that their commonness lent them a solemnity heretofore unknown to Gregs. His seventeenth floor apartment over-looked the Manhattan skyline to the south and from 86th Street, he could see the towers of the World Trade Center, in whose shadow he knew Mary was accomplishing these common but miraculous things, and he would laugh at himself and the way he was "trading," as he might say, "on dreams."

These dreams became the coinage of nightmare, in part, when he left for Seattle, worried that by the time he returned, some other, younger man at work to whom he'd once said, "If I were younger, I'd take Mary out," might have taken him too seriously and be doing just that, at that very moment. The way Mary had stood at the bottom of her stairs and looked at him as though he were an exceptionally edible food. The way she said, "Hey," and had taken his face in her endearing sausage fingers and kissed him goodnight while he was yet in the process of shuffling his feet and deciding whether he dared to kiss her. The way the skin between her neck and breast had looked unsullied and smooth, like freshly fallen snow, and yet burnished, like a marble relief. And the feel to his hand of the back of her neck, which stayed with the hand as though it had a will and memory of its own. All seemed out of a novel and not out of real life.

When he thought about the difference between novels and real life, Gregs led himself to the suspicion that she had done, was doing, these same things with that other younger man. In real life, that was what would happen. He knew that as well as he knew that all his life he had had to convince girls that he was worth falling in love with. He had always had to persist in battering down the walls of her resistance, buying it off, in a sense, with flowers, and dinners out, and small attentions to her quirks, anxieties, and problems—the little attentions that women seemed so sus-ceptible to. Though he had often expressed resentment at this fact of his life, he had always assumed that this was the way things were supposed to be, like having turkey and not goose for Christmas. Now, Mary seemed in control and, though pleased over the novelty of Mary's kissing him without solicitation, he was off guard and suspicious of Mary's quickness. Had he been able to, Gregs would have married her immediately.

"As if," he added, remembering his father's unshaken beliefs in fidelity—even after his experience with Anna, Barron's stepmother— "that would guarantee anything. Anything, at all."

Then, too, the nature of flight changed on him. Always before, he had enjoyed flying, enjoyed the pleasurable sensation and expectation as the plane's unwilling wheels left the ground and the plane soared upwards, leaving its noise and smoke in a trail behind it, up and up, to touch the hands of God. For the first time in his life, he discovered within himself a fear and hatred for flying, and he wondered where in hell this plane might make a water landing—for which his seat cushion could be used as a flotation device.

Additionally, his travel agency had booked him on an indirect flight that required three take-offs and three landings before he would be safely on the macadam in Seattle. Circling O'Hare, seeing several other jets in similar patterns out the window, he felt a claustrophobia as intense as that which he felt on the FDR highway in heavy rain. When a panel fell off the cabin ceiling upon landing in Chicago, and a main-tenance crew walked aboard and taped the panel back up with duct tape, Gregs found himself bitterly aware of his own mortality, and it forced him to reconsider one of his father's maxims, that plans were decoys for fools. Even the irony he normally would have noted regard-ing his father's will in the light of this maxim was buried in his visual and nearly tactile memory of Mary's neck.

After Chicago came Denver, a change of planes (during which, Gregs was certain, the airline had to lose his luggage), and finally, the immensity of Seattle, connected underground by a circular subway line. Having consumed nine drinks in flight, Gregs was somewhat calm and composed. Yet, when Harry greeted him and asked, "How was your flight?" all Gregs could say was, "Mortal," causing Harry to glance at him sideways, uncertain as to whether this was meant to be funny or not. They watched the first luggage bag emerge from underground on a conveyor belt, pause at the apex, and slide down on to the revolving hinged conveyor that displayed the arriving bags. The appearance of this first bag caused the crowd to mill forwards and Gregs moved back a few feet, believing his bags were lost, knowing the baggage handlers would wait several minutes before sending up the second bag. The handlers were perverse, and this first bag was merely a premonition which caused the crowd to crush together in an impossible anticipation.

"Plans," he said to Harry.

Despite the thermos of margaritas and the two bottles of chilled champagne Harry had brought along for the trip from Seattle to his stepmother's house, Gregs felt that his relationship with his half brother had changed, damaged irreparably, perhaps, by his comment about every bitch in heat. And Gregs felt awkward, trying to talk to him about marriage. After all, Harry was an expert on the subject. Nonetheless, each time Gregs broached the topic, Harry said something to close it off again, like, "Three's the charm" or "The end of the endless road."

In addition, they had stopped by the University of Washington to gather up Cheryl, Gregs's half sister, and her friend Janie. Cheryl had been all of a mother-hating fourteen years old when he'd moved east, so he felt he hardly knew her. Janie's presence on the occasion of his return to his father's fatherless house, he resented. On top of that, Janie was a yuppie's puppy, the child of an up and coming politico who happened to be in South America for the holidays. Charitably, Cheryl had dragged her along to her mother's home, so she—as well as Cheryl, herself—wouldn't be alone for the holidays.

Janie wore impressively tight designer jeans that separated her thighs as she walked and revealed a heart-shape of light between her legs, near her crotch—what Mary would have called a "tart"—and she and Cheryl seemed overly concerned with beer busts and boys, as they gabbled about ski weekends and fraternity parties.

Gregs did manage a monosyllabic politeness towards Janie, receding beneath the noise of their conversation long enough to wonder how in hell his father could have spawned someone so different from him and Harry as Cheryl seemed to have become. But then Harry was changed, too, and Gregs felt totally alone, wishing he had not come but had stayed in New York. His mind worked its way through all of the clichés about 'You can't go home again, and ended with 'father, father, why have you forsaken us?' Gregs thought he knew why, and it made him feel like screaming.

"What are you thinking?" Harry said.

"Upbringing," Gregs replied.

Janie had boingy hair, the kind which, put up behind her head, revolted against the scrunchy, releasing wisps of wild hair one at a time until it was all falling about her face in waterfalls of calculated disarray.

"I know what you mean," Harry said, sipping his champagne. "You oughtta have kids, yourself."

"Hmm," Gregs said. He had never wanted kids, always using the excuse that it was hard enough to establish yourself in this world without the albatross of children. As Edgerman, who had seven children, had said, "Every time I start to relax, one of my kids comes along and kicks the stool out from under me." Gregs had agreed. Kids were a burden. And yet now, having nowhere to go in the company, having achieved all he could for the time being, maybe kids were a possibility.

"I am thinking about getting married," he said to Harry, admitting the possibility, as though marriage and kids went together, like peanut butter and jam.

"So that's why you keep bringing marriage up," Harry said. "I thought you were trying to check up on me, all those indirect questions." He held out his champagne glass for Gregs to refill. "Kinda quick, isn't it? How long have you known her?"

Gregs had to think about it. He had known Mary for a matter of weeks. And yet, he'd been saying for some time the bit about 'if he were younger.' She'd worked for the company for a couple of years, too, and he'd seen her and talked with her several times over lunch.

"For a while," he said.

It was Harry's turn to say, "Hmmm."

By the time they pulled in behind his father's—Anna's—house, he had consumed enough champagne to feel warm and comfortable inside. The sight of the house had a negative effect, momentarily, like the little voice inside that was warning him about tomorrow's hang-over. The paint was peeling from the siding and the large, sloping yard was brown and uncared for, the chain-link fence surrounding it more intent on keeping the owners in and not the public out. It was a large house, and the largeness of its neglect was all the more expressive of the passivity his father had displayed more and more often, as he neared his unexpected death. To Gregs, it expressed a helplessness in the face of vicissitude. Like a riverbed without the river, it expressed a feeling for the river that had once been there, which now depressed Gregs with its undeniable absence.

Anna, too, fit into Gregs's depression. He had expected her to be thin and wan from the grief diet, as he called it. Instead, she was plumper than before, apparently cheerful, and it caused him to think, unpacking his bags in what had been his father's bedroom, that "death" ought to be replaced with "beds" in the marriage ceremony—"until beds do we part."

His father had always claimed that he was happy, and that the separate beds, and later the separate bedrooms, were a matter of convenience, a way in which his father and Anna could get a good night's sleep without being bothered by the tossing or snoring of the other person. Now, to Gregs, this bed became a symbol, and he tore the sheets and mattress pad from the bed, looking for a stain, a slight discoloration, that would prove that the bed had been used, but except for the tender infirmities of the springs in the mattress's middle, the bed may as well have been new. He was overwhelmed by what he imagined was the absence of comfort in his father's last years, and he staggered, catching his balance by grabbing at the night stand.

Whatever equanimity he had remaining to him was erased that afternoon and evening as he listened to the common chit-chat that passed between Anna, Cheryl, Harry and his fiancé, and Janie. Anna, he didn't blame, even though her cheerful façade failed to show the proper fissures of weakness and pain. He, himself, had come to know how he could be walking down 86th Street, happy and content, and suddenly, without cause, tears would start to fall from his eyes; how, at work, he might turn away from the person he was talking to, his face momentarily etched with loss, feeling silly.

In Anna, he detected none of these moments. Cheryl was young and evidently as dumb as a tuna in school. Harry's fiancé was sweet and agreeable, the kind of person whose common opinions lend a sort of seriousness to her triviality. You could forgive her avoidance of certain topics of conversation, tolerate it the same way a house full of former socialists might tolerate a republican. For the most part, Gregs kept himself secret, exulting in what he thought was controlled rage.

It was Janie who drove him away from the dinner table, on Christmas Eve.

Janie had appeared for dinner, the wisps of her hair brushed back into place, a fishnet blouse allowing glimpses of the flesh-colored bra as she passed the dishes or reached for her wine. Gregs spent most of the meal telling himself that Janie was a tart who would demand infinite patience if one were to get anywhere with her. He didn't want a woman like her. That was why he liked Mary.

And yet, as much as he told himself he didn't want this, he also had to admit that he was attracted to it. It was a part of his and Harry's nature, as though they had been brain-washed as children into believing that Janie was the apotheosis of femininity, that the only worthwhile challenge was to overcome Janie's measured coolness, to penetrate her non-committal flirtatiousness—to, in short, make her care.

Wondering about this, Gregs heard her tell Cheryl that she wouldn't marry her boyfriend, Todd, until after they had lived together for a long time.

"Otherwise," Janie said, smiling at Gregs, "How could I ever be sure someone else wouldn't come along, who I liked more?"

"Nothing," Harry said, "is permanent. Although some things are forever," he added, patting the hand of his fiancé.

"And some of the best," Janie said, "are the ones you know can't be permanent, because of circumstances."

"Like one night stands?" Cheryl said.

"Cheryl!" Anna said.

As calmly as possible, Gregs finished his wine, set his glass down, and excused himself.

"There's dessert," Anna said.

"Thanks, but I'm not hungry," Gregs said. "I feel a little sick, from the trip, so forgive me but I think I'll go up and lie down for a while."

He heard Harry's fiancé complain that he was going to get out of helping with the dishes, and Harry's weary voice promise her that he would do them.

"He's tired," Harry said.

Gregs closed the door to the bedroom; had there been a lock on the door, he would have locked it. He missed his father, terribly. He needed to talk to somebody.

He didn't feel a great deal better when Mary answered the phone and said, "Do you know what time it is?"

He had forgotten that the world he had left was functioning by a different clock and, as simple-minded as it might seem, it made him realize how different was the world he lived in from this western world of his half family.

"Sorry," he said. "I forgot. I missed you, and I forgot."

"Me too,"she said. Someone on her end said something. "It's Barron." She laughed.

"What's that?" he asked. "Nothing. My father's making jokes."

"What did he say?"

"Nothing," she said. "We were just talking about you. He likes you. Though he thinks you ought to change your name." She laughed again.

"Marry me," Gregs blurted, immediately surprised and embarrassed.

"Okay. Sure," she said. "Are you a little tipsy?"

"No," Gregs said, mustering whatever seriousness he could. "No, I'm not." He was angered by what he assumed was her implication that only drunkenness would have caused him to ask her to marry him.

"I've got to go," Mary said. "We'll talk when you get back. Merry Christmas."

"Do you have to go so soon?"

"It's my turn. We're in the middle of a Scrabble game. It's my turn. I'll talk to you later. Bye."

"Think about it," Gregs said as the phone line went dead. The hell with you, Gregs thought, more determined than ever that she would marry him.

It wasn't until Christmas dinner, for which Harry's fiancé had prepared an excellent ham, that Gregs realized what had been missing all those years in his family, and that was a center, some focal point which not only made the family come together but also to cohere. His father, it seemed to him, had tried, and had, in some ways, succeeded in forming a kind of flexible center. But that was what was missing, that inflexibility which, right or wrong, might focus the family by making it tolerate him. Gregs knew that he didn't mean that a father, or mother, should be always inflexible. Yet, like Harry, in his need to get along with everyone in the family, his father had adopted a backward bending attitude which allowed him to bend at the wrong times, in the wrong places—allowed, in a sense, the goose, instead of the traditional turkey—a slightly mushy attitude that theoretical liberals might admire, but which expressed itself in his stepmother's sleeping in a separate bed from his father. All these years, Gregs had been telling himself that though they slept in separate beds, they did so out of convenience and the need for undisturbed sleep. Now, he wasn't so certain that that was the truth. "Until beds do us part," he thought, laughing to himself. Suddenly, Gregs saw the suffering his father must have endured, and he understood.

At the same moment, Cheryl said to Janie, "Sex isn't everything."

"The hell it's not," he said, looking dangerously at Cheryl, daring her to contradict him. He was aware of how everyone at the table had ceased the motions of eating and was staring at him.

"Barron," Harry said. "What's the matter with you?"

"Yes, Barron," Anna said. "Could we manage to keep the conversation polite?"

"Tasteful?" Gregs sneered, remembering how Mary had said that fashions had to be both exquisite and tasteful—the latter to convince the baggage in the audience that they, too, could look like the models.

"If you like," Anna said.

"Fuck tastefulness," he said. "Tastefulness is just a way of ignoring the truth, a way of you convincing yourselves that you aren't what you aren't. A way for little Cheryl, here, to seem more intelligent than a tuna fish, or a way for Janie to convince herself that she likes Todd, even though she wants to keep the bedroom door open."

"Harry," Harry's fiancé said.

"And you. My god. 'He's going to get out of doing the dishes.' That's what you were whining about last night, isn't it? Have you ever just done anything for someone without needing a balance sheet? No. No, you'll be just like all of Harry's wives and . . ."

"What matters . . . ," she began.

"This!" he shouted, jumping up and grabbing his crotch. "This is what matters!"

"Barron," Harry said.

"And you, Harry. . . ." He stopped, looking into a face that he had loved and which now looked a lot like his own father's face the time he had dared, as a young man, to question the reasons for his father's existence.

"And you," he said, nodding. "I love you, Harry," he said quietly. "I'm sorry. But I don't see why you want to marry a girl whose greatest disappointment in life was not making the cheerleading squad."

Harry's fiancé coughed decorously, like someone who thinks she's just swallowed the fly in her drink, as Barron fled the room.

V.

IN DEFENSE OF BARRON GREGS, WHO WAS REALLY ACTING LIKE AN ASS-hole, we might offer up his distress over his father's death, especially as this was his first Christmas without his father. We could also say that, though he was secretly defiant because he believed he had told the truth, he felt awful for having spoiled his family's Christmas, and embarrassed them all in front of both Harry's fiancé and Janie.

For most of his thirty odd years, he had lived tastefully, himself, pur-suing women with the casual belief that nothing was forever and that change was inevitable. Barron believed himself to be willing to change. What he had not been prepared for, and which caused his little tantrum at the dinner table, was the notion that he had never changed at all, that all the women he had pursued looked and acted a lot alike—the Julies and Janies and Jills. Proof of this, he found in the mere fact that most of his former girlfriends had had names, oddly enough, beginning with J. Even chasing women had become such a part of his routine that he had never really been alone, even at the times he was uninvolved.

Whether or not it was his decision to try marriage, or his having run across a family as different as Dubrovnik from the town he'd grown up in that changed him, we don't know.

We do know that Cheryl never spoke to him again, and Anna only spoke with him on the phone, settling the details of his giving up his share of his father's estate to her in an act, as Anna saw it, of contrition for his behavior. Gregs was not contrite.

Harry, the most courageous of anyone, forgave Barron, even though after fighting bitterly with his fiancé about his half brother's words on Christmas, defending Barron's right to explode and still be tolerated, his fiancé jumped ship. He was even able to laugh about the incident when he visited New York to attend his half brother's wedding reception.

"She said she couldn't marry into a family that tolerated language like that at the dinner table."

Gregs looked perplexed.

"She meant 'fuck'," Harry said. "She hates the word almost as much as doing it."

"It's a problem," Gregs said. "Almost as important as what to have for a holiday dinner."

"Not for you, I see," Harry said.

When Harry teased his brother, alluding to his quick courtship and marriage, Gregs smiled self-consciously and said, "I figure that nothing's forever," and they both laughed over that, even though Harry could see that Gregs believed that while nothing may be forever, some things might be permanent. How similar Gregs was, in some ways, to their father, Harry thought. And yet, how unlike him, too. It was the only hope for either of them.

"Can we talk?" Harry said.

"Sure," Gregs said. "Only later. There's somebody I want to introduce you to. She used to work for me."

He dragged Harry over to meet Julie Askew who, displaying some courage of her own, had come to the reception.

"She's no cheerleader," he said, leaving then, alone. Though she was stinking drunk, she and Harry hit it off and following Gregs's example, Harry took Julie with him, back to the Hyatt, where he was staying and where Gregs had booked the honeymoon suite.

"So, what do you think of my new family?" Gregs asked Harry, as the two couples strolled up the avenue at midnight, looking for a delicatessen.

"Different," Harry said, causing Mary to look at Gregs, and laugh.

Neither Mary nor Gregs ever mentioned the Christmas party to Harry, and they were fairly certain, when they discussed it, that Julie hadn't either.

"What matters," Mary would say, "is that it doesn't matter."

Gregs was grateful for Mary's attitude. It made him believe that everything, anything could be forgiven.

Three months later, Harry and Julie were married, and the two couples became friends, able to disagree among the four of them as vehemently as any one of them with his partner. Sometimes, Harry worried about what Julie and Mary might talk about. Gregs never did, no more than Mary worried over what he and Harry might say to each other. Even when Mary confessed that she had told her parents which boss had taken Julie Askew home from that inimical party, Gregs didn't really mind. Besides, it was too late, he was a part of the family, now.

Sometimes, drunk and feeling sentimental, Gregs asks Mary if she was shocked by his asking her to marry him so quickly, not to mention over the phone, and Mary says, "No, I knew you'd get around to it."

Though he has wondered whether Mary was in control all along, Gregs pursues the topic no farther than that, realizing that a little mystery can go a long ways. And when Mary inquires as to why her husband decided to lay off Julie Askew the week before Harry arrived to attend their reception, Gregs grins and says something about its being like a little death.

"It kept things," he says, "from being too much like a novel."